Avenged

Book 7 of A New Life Series

Samantha Jacobey

Avenged

Book 7 of A New Life Series

Samantha Jacobey

Lavish Publishing, LLC ~ Houston

Table of Contents

Prologue

Eli cast a glance to his left, his partner towering above him as they marched to their sedan. "You know this is only going to get more complicated," he spoke crisply, relieved to be outside the building.

"Yes, it is," the other man agreed. "So, if you have any doubts, this is the time to speak up." Mason kept moving as he cajoled, reaching for the door handle and climbing inside.

Taking his place behind the wheel, Eli started the car and pulled away from the curb, moving a few hundred yards and parking again to wait. "You don't know her like I do," he stated flatly. "She's a compulsive liar. Only gives you enough truth to make her story sound credible."

Mason cut his gaze over at him, "Is that your ego talking?"

Drumming his fingers on the wheel, he considered the question, "I don't know. Maybe. She got the better of me, and two agents have paid the price with their lives. Three counting the one she killed when she was still with the Dragons."

"I'm going with her," his passenger cut in. "Regardless of what you think, that's the side I'm choosing. If you want to play it by the book, I will understand. But know this: James Godfry is dirty. I can't prove it, yet. But I will."

Bending his arm, Eli slouched over and rested his elbow

on the door frame, his head in his hand as if he had a migraine. "I'm tired of thinking about it. Half a decade. That's how long I've been worrying about this. Trying to figure it out."

"Stop trying so hard," Mason offered. "What's your gut telling you?"

"My *gut*?" the other man sneered, "The last time I listened to anything other than my head, I wound up reassigned. Still haven't figured out how they discovered what happened between us, either. I figure Tori talked once she was done with me." He could hear the rumble start low, turning his head to see Agent Hunt trying to suppress his laughter. "What's so fucking funny?"

"You," his counterpart continued to snicker. "I shouldn't laugh though. It took me a while to figure it out." Shifting in his seat, Mason drew a deep breath to calm his spasms, "Debra was sleeping with Godfry. I'm sure she mentioned it to him, maybe not even thinking anything of it."

"You're kidding me! How the hell did you find that out?"

"I poked around... a lot," Hunt shrugged. "Found out quite a few interesting things about the Chicago office," he dusted imaginary dirt off his knee for a moment. "The only reason I trust you, is because Tori says I can."

Eli's brow furrowed, "What the hell does that mean? You'd take her word over mine?"

"You could say that." Mason opened his left palm to the roof, "Let me clue you in on my theory about people. I don't put much stock in what people say. Everyone's a liar. Everyone hides the truth and covers their ass at some point in their lives. You want to know who someone is... what they stand for... watch what they do. They'll tell you who they are."

Mason turned enough to look the other man in the eye. "Don't judge her too harshly. In the end, she's the one who holds the key to ending this whole mess. That's a lot of weight for one pair of shoulders to bear. Besides, she didn't choose to leave you. She was holding on the best she could until she found out you were gone. That's when things fell apart."

"Yeah," Eli scoffed, "Tell me about it," leaning back into his palm with a sigh.

Get the Hell Out

Tori glanced around the shop, her lips drawn into a frown. *Son of a bitch.* She didn't want to be there. Didn't want things to have turned out the way they were. "You think the car is back yet?"

"I'll check," Brett offered calmly, leaving his cohorts in the back and making his way out to the single glass door next to the register. Pushing it open enough to glance up and down the street, he then allowed it to close, relocking it with a snap.

"Nope. Not back yet," he sighed the words when he had rejoined the others. "We should make a plan, what we're gonna do when it does get here." Glancing between the other two men, he continued, "You're in charge, baby girl. That means it's up t' you."

"This isn't a dictatorship," she tossed at him flatly, sinking down to sit on the edge of Terry's workbench.

"It ain't a democracy, neither," he replied calmly. "It's ok, tell us what you think. If we don't like it, we'll let ya know."

The girl inhaled deeply, pushing the air out noisily through a relaxed jaw, "Alrighty then." She gave them her evaluation, "We're pretty much fucked. All our bikes are scattered across the country, so we have no rides. The Organization knows everything about us, and we have almost no information on them -"

"Stop bein' negative," Brett cut her off.

"Why?" she snapped. "I'm so fucking pissed off, I can't even see straight!" her fists were clenched in her lap as she vented.

"Then take a deep breath," he stepped closer to her, his hand catching her jaw and lifting it slightly. "That's it," his thumb caressed her cheek, "Don' be angry. Be smart. We can beat these guys. You know more about 'em than you think."

Tori blinked up at him, relaxing into his touch. "We can buy some motorcycles locally; I think that'll be our best option. We don't have access to much cash," her mind began to branch out. "How much was in the vault? The one here in LA?" Brett grinned, reaching inside his jacket for his list.

"Well, we inventoried 'em all, so le's see what this one has for us..." his voice trailed away as he scanned the page. "Over 400K. We could get some really nice bikes for that an' still have some t' carry aroun'.''

She blinked a few times at the news. "Why did they burn the house? It doesn't make sense. They should have come to the hotel. They should have come after me."

"We'll figure it out," Michael tried to reassure her. "Brett's right. For the moment, we need to know what we're going to do. Where should we go to hole up? I don't think the hotel is a good option. Not in the long run."

"We have to separate ourselves from the group," Tori agreed, continuing his thought. "Yes, we go back to the hotel. Whatever we do needs to be dramatic and public. We need those snapping the pictures to get plenty of them so that everyone knows we aren't with the band anymore. Let's go out front, so we can leave as soon as the car gets here."

Making their way to the single glass door, Tori leaned against it, waiting impatiently for the limo. Moving up behind her, Michael ran his hand up her spine, squeezing her shoulder at the top. Turning, she leaned into his embrace and avoided looking at the others, hoping they didn't have long to wait.

A few minutes later, the front of the car pulled up into view, and the four of them slipped out. Tori instructed Derrick to lock the door behind them and go home, closing the shop as a precaution. The young man obeyed, not knowing any of the details, but certain it meant trouble; trouble he wanted no part in.

Inside the limo, Brett took the center seat across from the bar, while Michael and Enrique sat on either side of their newly appointed leader. "I want you two to stop fighting over me," she stared at the floor in front of her, her words sharp.

"Fighting over you?" Enrique sounded perplexed.

"Yeah, fighting," she cut her eyes over at him, "I see the way you give each other dirty looks and do shit to one-up each other. I want you to cut that shit out. We have no time for that crap. If we're all going, then we all have to be respected... respected and respectful. No infighting. Like Mason said, the enemy is out there."

Reaching over to take her hand, Michael agreed, "You're exactly right, baby girl. And I'm one-hundred-percent for it." To his surprise, she pulled her hand away, shifting the glare to him.

"Then I'll let you know when you can touch me." Getting up from her seat, she moved to the opposite end of the car, sitting with her back to the driver and staring out the window.

Leaving her alone, the group remained silent until they drew close to the hotel. Then the girl began to give orders. "When we get upstairs, we pack. I'm going to start a fight with the rest of the guys. Pack two changes of clothes and call a cab." She turned her attention to Brett, "You and Enrique retrieve the money from the vault. Meet us at the airport. You," she frowned at her husband, "Get our stuff together and have the plane ready to go. File a flight plan for Florida. We should be in and out of here in thirty minutes."

She gave them their directions, not expecting any argument, and not getting any. When they reached the hotel, she calmly led the way to the elevator. Once inside, the three men stood behind her, Tori staring at her reflection in the glossy metal, mentally preparing herself to play the role of angry bitch from hell; not much of a stretch as of late.

The shiny doors parted, and the three men went into their rooms while Tori made her way down the hall, trying to decide what she would say to begin the argument. It turned out, she needn't have worried about that part because the fight would take care of itself.

Entering her brother's room, she stopped cold at the sight of the young blonde, standing next to his window and admiring the view, "Lindsey? What the hell are you doing here?!?" her voice exploded with accusation.

Giving her a weak smile, the girl smoothed her hair, "Hey, Tori," being all she could manage as a reply.

"Wait," Brian held up a hand to intervene, "This is my fault. I know you didn't want me seeing her -"

Throwing her palms up, Tori cut him off, "You bet this is your fault! Get some fucking clothes together, right now! Two changes and don't argue." Glaring over at the girl, she raised her eyebrow, "You have any clothes with you? Let me guess… only what you have on."

Lins hung her head, nodding slightly, "I guess you're pretty unhappy with me."

"Later," Tori shot back at her, "Right now, I have to figure out how to keep you from ending up dead."

Brian spun around from digging through his clothes, gaping at her. "Why'd you say that?" he demanded.

"Because you're two of the most important people on

earth to me. I intended to leave you here, but now I think we need to take you with us. At least for the time being. Go on and get your stuff together. I need to go start a fight with Cody and Collin." Giving Lindsey one last shake of her head, she exited the suite and made her way down the hall, locating Collin's door and pounding on it loudly.

"Open the God damned door!" she screamed at the top of her voice.

Instantly, the portal swung wide before her; his chin raised as he shouted back, "What the fuck're you doin'?!?"

"Creating an alibi," she replied calmly as she pushed past him and began to knock things over in the room, relieved to find him alone. Grabbing a lamp, she smashed it against the wall, bellowing, "You son of a bitch! You can't talk to me that way!"

Collin only stared at her, dumbfounded.

Giving him a circular motion with her hand, she dropped her voice as she sidled towards him, "Collin honey, you have to play along. Scream at me. Anything."

"Why?" he demanded, "What's going on?"

Tori bit her lip, "Remember the bad guys I was worried about?" He nodded, so she continued, "They burned the halfway house to the ground last night."

"Holy shit! Are your friends ok?"

"Yeah, but we have to move fast. That's why you have to go with me here. We have a fight, and the guys and I are going to Florida. You and Cody go back to Jersey and stay there. Make sure Pete takes care of you – don't let anything happen to you, ok?"

"Ok," he nodded, his mouth suddenly dry as he attempted to swallow. "You're such a stupid bitch!" he screamed. "I don't know what the hell we were thinking, asking you to play with us!" Reaching over, he lifted the elegant nightstand and sent it crashing into the doorframe.

The couple carried on for several minutes, until security showed up to escort them outside. Holding up her hands, Tori held onto the façade, "Hey, hey, it's ok, I was leaving anyway!" Tossing her bandmate an angry glare, she stormed out of the room, making her way down the hall. Her brother fell in beside her, carrying his bag and working to keep up. As they strode onto the elevator, she inquired in French, "All set?"

"Yeah, everyone's down in the car," he nodded, pushing the button.

"Good," she shook her dark waves, "Remember to look pissed when we step out."

He snickered, "I'll try."

Lightening quick, she punched him in the chest, "Maybe you need a little motivation. Why the fuck didn't you listen to me?" She glared at him, no hint of a smile on her drawn features.

His grin removed, he blinked at her, "I dunno," and the doors opened.

Stepping out into the lobby, several flashes went off as the pair exited the small space, and the girl held her hand up, as if she were trying to block them from photographing her. With angry long strides, the two made their way out front and climbed into the long black car, breathing a sigh of relief.

"Airport," she muttered.

"Yeah, we're on it," Michael supplied calmly.

"Good. Give me your cell phone," Tori held her hand out towards her brother.

"Why? Who're you gonna call?" he asked as he dug the device out of his pocket.

"No one," she replied crisply, "But you can't take it with you. It has to go with us, so people think we're still together."

His brow furrowed, "That doesn't make any sense, sis."

"Sure it does. Cell phones are extremely unsecure. People can listen in on your conversations and can use them to locate you." He stared at her, mouth hanging open in surprise.

"They can really do that?" Lindsey appeared dazed.

Tori glanced calmly over at her young friend, nodding slowly, "Yeah, they can do that. That's why I'm taking the phone with me. You guys are going to Texas. When we leave on the plane, you two take a cab to the bus station. Get on a bus and head to our place. Stay there. Out of the way."

"Is that why you never wanted one?" he queried, his mind still stuck on the phone.

"Yes," she replied coolly. "And remember not to use your credit card. It will be cash only."

"I don't have any cash," he countered.

"You will. Brett and Enrique will meet us at the airport. They will have plenty - twenty thousand for you. It should be enough since you'll be hiding at our house." She didn't smile, and he could tell she wasn't happy about the situation.

"I'm sorry I didn't listen to you," he whispered in their alternate language, staring at her hands, unable to look her in the eye.

"It's too late for that. Take care of Lins, that's all you can do," she replied in kind. Switching to English, she gave her friend a weak smile, "Do what he says, ok? My brother's gonna look after you, make sure you're safe."

"Yeah," the girl nodded, fear in her eyes. "Michael told me what's going on," she smiled at her friend's mate, "We'll be ok."

Heaving a deep sigh, Tori leaned back into the seat, the adrenaline still coursing through her veins. It would help her fight her fatigue for a while, but eventually she would crash. *Maybe on the plane I can catch a nap.*

16

Set Up Shop

Things went smoothly as the group arrived at the airport and made their way to the private jet. Enrique and Brett had met them at the entrance, carrying a duffel bag containing the money. Once they were cleared and on the plane, Tori opened it, her actions swift as she pulled out a stack of bills, fanning it to count out about twenty thousand for her brother.

"Here," she shoved the wad at him, "Don't spend it all in one place."

Taking the cash in one hand, he threw the other arm around her, "Be safe. How will we know everything's ok?"

"We have a phone in the house, remember? And don't go contacting a bunch of people. The fewer who know where you are, the better," her voice cracked as she spoke. "I still love you, Danny. And I'm not mad. Just disappointed."

"I know," he stroked her hair. "And don't worry. We'll be fine." Putting an end to the goodbye, he reached for Lindsey's fingers, "You and me, kid," his voice crisp, he guided her off the plane.

Tori watched them go with a heavy heart. "You three take the front seats. I'd like to be alone for a while," she stipulated as she fastened herself into one of the back seats and stared out the portal to her right. She was asleep before the plane had leveled out.

The three men noted her slumped condition, and Brett spoke up, "For almost two weeks she's been runnin' on fumes. I'd have thought by now one o' you would've backed off."

Both men peered over at him, not sure what to make of the comment.

"You think we're wearing her out, do you? Just the two of us?" Michael sneered, "You forget where she came from," his fingers grazed the underside of his chin.

"So you're pleadin' innocent, then," the older man countered.

Michael shifted in his seat, so that he could see his wife's face while she dozed, "Pretty much. This is something else. I'm not going to speculate what." Pulling his eyes back to the other men, "Suffice it to say, she isn't well. We need to keep that in mind as this... situation unfolds."

Enrique agreed with a simple nod, bothered that he couldn't see her for himself. "I haven't touched her. And not for lack of trying, minds you." He grinned at the few times he had been able to put his hands on her, "But she's pretty stubborn."

The three shared in the chuckle at their girl being strong willed.

"Alright, then le's all get some rest while we can," Brett commanded, assuming he would be her second, and in the position to give orders.

The group awakened shortly before they landed at the airport in Miami, and Tori joined the three of them in the front section of seats, "Thanks, guys, I really needed that." She smiled, noticing that they had taken advantage of the opportunity as well.

"So, where's this place that we're going to, exactly," Enrique inquired with an exaggerated stretch.

"Fort Lauderdale," she supplied. "Brian has a house there, which we're going to borrow. I figure we can stay three days at most, but after that we need to move on. We don't want to be found by anyone on the other side. I'm also concerned about how we're going to contact Eli and Mason. Why couldn't he give us his number?" she muttered the question, more or less, to herself.

"Having second thoughts about trusting him?" he probed.

Tori didn't reply and shifted her gaze over at him as anger boiled up unexpectedly inside her. Drawing a deep breath to control it, she clenched her teeth, "Was I that convincing, back at the shop?"

His jaw dropped, "You means you don't really trust him?"

Emitting a loud giggle, Tori looked over at her husband and shook her head. "We've had this conversation before, haven't we, love. No, I don't, but there wasn't any need tipping him off to that fact, either. Not to mention that the other one, Mason Hunt, contacted me before we left for LA."

"He did what?" Michael coughed loudly in surprise, sitting up straighter, "When the hell was this?" He rarely let the woman out of his sight, so he could hardly imagine them carrying on secret conversations.

"After Christmas, the day I was sick, and I left you guys in the lounge early in the evening. I snuck out the window and met him in a bar," she confessed, not exactly proud of her actions.

Michael stared at her, his mind running through the particular night in question, until he arrived at the end of it. "And all the two of you did was talk, huh?"

She held her husband's gaze, refusing the desire to look away, "Yeah, all we did was talk. He told me they were watching us, and that I was in danger."

"And you didn' think this was worth mentionin'?" Brett interceded.

Tori hung her head, the urge too great to ignore any longer. "What was I supposed to do, tell you guys that the

Feds were tailing us and expected us to be attacked at any moment?"

"Wells it was pretty fucking irresponsible for you not to," Enrique chimed in.

She looked up, her face drawn, on the verge of tears at having the three of them coming at her at once. "You know, you guys are free to go anytime you damn well please. I can handle this by myself. This was intended to be a one woman job to begin with." Standing, she moved back to the second set of seats, taking one that faced the back of the plane.

The men of the group sat staring at one another for a full minute before Michael rose calmly. Making his way around to the back, he kneeled down in front of his bride. Laying his hand on hers with a gentle touch, he peered up into her crystal blue orbs, "The secrets stop here. You said it yourself; we can't be effective if we can't be respectful, and keeping things from each other isn't conducive to that. As soon as we get to the house, we're going to have a long conversation and clear the air."

He took his place next to her, maintaining his hold on her while the plane landed. Gathering their gear, he carried her bag, as well as his own, refusing to relinquish his grip on her in the meantime. Catching a cab, they arrived at the house an hour later, and it occurred to him that no one had spoken since he made his little speech on the plane.

Allowing the two Scorpions to go up and choose rooms, Michael and Tori made their way to the kitchen to arrange for their dinner. Maria appeared surprised by their arrival, and even more so that the property's owner had not been with them. However, she did her best to accommodate them, and began to prepare a meal for them to enjoy.

Making their way into the lounge, with its cheerful red furnishings ready to warm their spirits, they waited for the other two men, surrounded by a strained silence. As soon as they were ready, Michael dove in, "Ok, love; we need specifics on your meeting. And, I don't want you to think I or we are angry at you," he gave the pair a glare. "We haven't been exactly honest with you either, so there's no point in making accusations of any kind."

Tori's clear blue eyes opened wider at his admission. She had suspected their secrecy after the discussion the group had held in the shop before they left LA. "Alright," she agreed in a submissive tone. "I might as well tell you. He caught me on my morning run. Said we needed to talk and gave me the location on a note."

"After I got away from you guys," she flicked her gaze between them nervously, "I met with him for less than an hour, then went back home. During the conversation, he told me that they fully expected The Organization to make a move against me. He also offered me a position on their team if I would agree to help them." She could see her husband grow tense at the news.

"I refused his offer, and he called me naïve. Said I should watch my back, and I left. I went home, and you know the rest." She stared at the floor as she finished, hoping her mate would not make a scene over her behavior after her shower. To her relief he did not.

"So basically, he didn't give you anything new, he merely wanted to see if they could recruit you; again." Michael kept his tone even.

"Yes," Tori agreed.

"Then I have a confession for you," he half smiled, "Enrique and I met up with Eli the first day we were in LA."

Tori's eyes shot up to meet his. "What does 'met up with' mean exactly?" she demanded, unable to be as cool as her mate.

"We… had coffee," he shrugged, recalling how they had badgered him. "He had been following us and we caught him in the coffee shop across the street from the studio. You and the guys were inside making the promos, so Enrique and I interrogated him. He claimed something had happened, and he was worried about you, and that's why he was there. But, we didn't buy it."

"I thinks he knew the attack was coming," Enrique interrupted, "From the way he was acting and what he said at the shop, about that guy Doug."

"Yeah," Michael agreed quickly, "He knew. And you were only saying that you trust him? You really don't?"

Tori caught her breath, taking a seat on a bar stool, considering the games she had always played with people. "It's complicated. You know, I've never tried to explain it to anyone; this vibe I get from people. I never thought anyone would take me seriously."

"But, when I'm dealing with other people, I feel like I can tell… about them. If they are being honest, or what their motives are. I don't always get it, but when I do, it's always right." She exhaled loudly, "And I get that nervous ache in my stomach before anything bad happens. No, sorry, that's not true. When I get the feeling, something bad happens, but I don't always get it."

Brett laughed, and Tori glared at him. Shrugging, he tried to keep a straight face, "So you're a witch after all."

Her face wrinkled, her temper short, she snapped "After all?"

He and Enrique made eye contact, and Enrique took over, "It's nothing," he shrugged. "We talked about you once; about how I thought you's a witch."

"You're making fun of me," her lip puckered into a pout. "I knew I shouldn't have told you."

"Its fine, love," Michael intervened. "Ignore these two," he wafted his hand between them, "Tell me about Eli."

Her blue orbs sullen, she complied, "Well, like I said,

he's complicated. When I'm around him, I get the feeling that he does care about me, at least most of the time. But then I get these odd, random vibes, like he's manipulating me, or trying to."

Enrique grew tense, his thoughts conflicted before he decided to divulge what he knew. "Wells, if you're looking for dirt on the guy… I knows a thing or two."

"Yeah," Michael pointed a crooked finger at him haphazardly. "You said before that he gave you some grief." Hearing an evil laugh from the dark haired man, the digit withdrew, "Well did he or didn't he?"

"Oh, he did," Enrique confirmed, "He sent me t' kills you."

"Sent you to kill him? When the fuck was this?" Tori bit in a fury.

"I dunno exactly," he replied calmly, "I's hanging around here and there, avoiding the Scorpions mostly, when I gets a call from him. I didn't know his name then, but he was the guy who put me in the halfway house." He could see her face grow more contorted, "Yeah, I left that part out before, didn't I."

"He put me there, and I was supposta meet up with the Scorpions and provides intel on them," he pulled out the phone that he had carried with him since LA. "Guess I'm not any good at taking orders from scrawny Feds, cause I didn't dos that, either. He gave me this at the time, then he calls me on it later to sends me after you." He shifted his gaze to stare at the other man, who remained silent.

"Anyways," he dropped his jaw, rolling his tongue for a moment. "His number's in here." Holding the device towards her, he waited for the girl to take it.

Her fingers trembling, she grasped it, and recalled having held it before. She had carried it while she repaired Geek's bike, and had used it to contact the Scorpions when the two of them were ready to rally with the group in Vegas; she had never suspected what it contained.

"What a mess," her voice deflated, "Can't any of us be trusted?" Flipping the unit open, she scrolled through the short list of numbers, finding the one that belonged to Eli. Inhaling deeply, she gave her command, "I'm going to call them in the morning, and tell them join us, here in the house."

"Jus' like that?" Brett tossed out, his eyes darting around the group. "He don' sound like anyone we need."

"Yes," Tori slapped the phone closed and shoved it in her pocket, "We're all liars and manipulators. There isn't a person among us who has been completely honest." She clenched her jaw, preparing for a fight, "Tell me I'm wrong."

She had grown stiff, her eyes darting from man to man. They each had their secrets and had done their share of coercion. At their failure to argue, she finished, "We convene this crew. Put our heads together and come up with a plan."

Tori lifted her chin, her eyes squinting slightly, "If you have any doubts, now is the time to walk away." Turning her back on them, she made her way to the kitchen to see about their dinner.

Time to Think

Eli stared at his phone in surprise, his hand trembling slightly as he lifted it with a crisp, "Hello?"

"Good morning!" Tori's voice sounded upbeat, "We need you. I guess you know where we are?"

"Of course," he replied evenly. "But I don't think it's a good idea. Like you said, we don't want to have the Bureau interfering until it becomes necessary." He cut his eyes over at the man next to him.

"It's necessary," her voice dropped. "How soon can you be here?"

"We'll be inside in a few minutes," he breathed, ending the call. "We've been requested to join them," he informed the other man calmly.

"Have you decided that's your move then?" Mason asked as he reached for the door handle.

"Yes," Eli replied, exiting the vehicle himself. "I'm not sure how it's going to play out, but I'm going to give it my best." The pair made their way up the path, leaving their vehicle in its secluded location. Arriving at the entrance, Eli knocked briskly, and Enrique opened the door almost immediately.

Stepping into the living area, the agent admired the glass surfaces, his eyes making their way over to the tall ebony haired woman who stood gazing out across the lake. The three men in the room fell back away from them, hands clasped as if they were waiting to be instructed.

"That was fast," the girl stated calmly.

"Yes, we arrived right behind you. We've been waiting outside for a few hours," Mason spoke for them.

"You should stay out of this," she cautioned the taller man, shifting so that her gaze fell on the floor slightly behind her twisted form.

Playing with his fingers, his mind raced, "What exactly is going on here?" he ignored the advice.

Turning to face them more fully, Tori's eyes bore into the man she had once thought the world of. Her lips beginning to curl, her grin became anything but calming, "I'm glad you could join us, Eli."

Sensing that something was wrong, her target shifted, taking half a step back as his gaze swept around the room. "I'm glad to be here," he lied flatly.

Bursting into laughter, she sneered, "You know what Eli is when you rearrange the letters?" She reached over and slid the glass door open, clearing the path to the deck, "We need to come to an understanding, don't we Eli. A real one."

Enrique stepped up behind the smaller man, giving him a shove towards the open door.

"Let's take this outside," she said calmly, "No need to ruin the furnishings." She ran her hand along the back of a white stuffed chair as he moved past her, Enrique close behind to continue the prodding.

"I think I warned you before," Eli bit his words sharply, glaring at him over his shoulder, "Touching me is assault."

Michael pounced, catching him with a right hook and knocking him through the open frame, "And we told you we aren't scared of that."

Eli fell onto the wooden beams, stumbling as he went down, the three of them filing out behind to encircle him.

"What the hell are you doing?" he cried out, looking

around for his partner, who was standing next to Brett, both men observing the proceedings.

Skipping forward, Tori kicked him in the chin, causing blood to spew out of his mouth, "See? I told you I didn't wanna mess up the furniture." Her boot caught him in the ribs on the next swing, a stab of guilt wrenching her gut at the pleasure of punishing him. "You're not much of a man, Eli," she looked him in the eye, clenching her fists and glaring at him.

His fingers wiped at the blood on his face. He then rolled over on his back, half sitting up, "Would you like to tell me why you're doing this?" His calm seemed out of place, and she held up her hand to signal the others to stop. Moving forward, she squatted down in front of him.

"Well, I can say one thing for you," she didn't smile, "You can take a beating. We're tired of the games, Eli. That means it's time to set things straight. We need to know that we can trust you. We need to be sure what team you're really on."

He frowned, "Are you kidding me? You're the one who said you did, remember?" His eyes darted to his hand, then down at the red splotches on his shirt. She didn't move while his chest began to heave more visibly. "What is it that you want from me?" he demanded a little more forcefully.

"I want the truth, Eli. Right here, right now, you start talking."

"About what? Ask me, and I'll tell you whatever you want to know," his eyes watched without blinking as she removed the knife from her boot and flicked it open.

"HEY!" Mason took a step forward, and the back of Michael's hand smacked him in the chest. Jerking his head over to glare at the sandy-haired man, he stood still, noticing the slow shake of his head.

"Don' worry, hun; Eli's gonna be fine. We need t' get us

a li'l understandin', tha's all," Tori dipped into a southern drawl, toying with him by turning the knife so that the morning sun glinted off of it and into his eyes. Dropping the accent, she continued, "You start talking, and I'm going to listen. If you tell me anything I don't like, I'm going to drop your body in the lake when we leave."

Eli stared at her, pulse in his throat. "You're not giving me much incentive," he breathed after a lengthy pause.

"So I should stick you and be done with it?"

His jaw dropped, and the pain in his chest broke through to the surface, leaking into his voice, "I never imagined you would speak to me that way."

"I'm a cold-hearted bitch, Eli. A murdering whore. I have been since you met me. The one thing that I have always tried to be, was honest, for as much as I could be." She inhaled deeply, "I only wish you could have been the same for me."

"You know I never had a choice," he replied calmly, "Neither of us did. You had your role to play, and I had mine." He glanced over at her husband, who had removed his arm from the shirt of his partner. "Even if we hadn't, there really wasn't much we had in common." He looked back at her, to see that she was chewing her lip. "Shall I go on?"

"Of course," she closed the knife with a snap.

"When you were in the hospital, and I was trying to get information, I said what I had to say to make that happen. What I didn't say, was how I got what I wanted, but it left me empty. I wanted something I was never meant to have. I wanted you, and not for a one night stand." He sat up straight, "I'm sorry I allowed things to go as far as they did."

"I'm here to help you finish this. I know you don't believe me, and you have every right to be angry," he dropped his eyes to take in his shirt again. "And if you were to feed me to the fishes, I really wouldn't blame you." Tori

28

snickered slightly at the phrase, and he smiled broadly, "Did I ever tell you that I loved you?"

"You have no right to say that!" her eyes flashed blue flames.

"I know," his voice remained steady. "I didn't mean it like that. What I meant was, I don't remember if I ever put it into words. So much has happened, and I'm sure you've figured out much of what I've done; how far I was willing to go to get you to do… this job." She squinted, and he held up a hand, "You have to know this is what I… I mean we, have been trying to get you to do all along."

"Yes, I know that it is."

"Then you answer a question for me. Why are you doing it?" He stared at her, listening to her silence for a full minute before he continued, "If you're such a cold hearted bitch, why not go back to the life you were raised to live? You have to know that The Organization would be happy to have you, with your skill set."

She still didn't respond, and he couldn't read anything on her placid features. "That's all I can tell you, Tori," his voice became quiet. "Until you tell me why you made this choice, that's all I have to say to you."

She drew in a deep breath and blew it out through her nostrils angrily, "Because I *don't* have a choice," she snapped. "They are attacking people I care about. There was a point, I thought I could run away; that I could hide, and that would protect them. But as time went on, I realized that Terry was right. There are always going to be people. That means I have to end this. I have to figure out how I'm supposed to do that, and I have to make sure that it's done."

He nodded, swallowing visibly, "The Organization didn't set the fire."

Tori fell back, sitting on her rear end, staring at him with her mouth wide open. "What the hell do you mean they didn't set the fire? Who the fuck did?" She had previously questioned the act herself, but having him throw the information at her was like a slap in the face.

"I don't know for sure. We have some other leads, and I'm fairly certain it wasn't them. That doesn't mean they weren't going to come after you, but they hadn't done it yet," he leaned forward, hanging his head slightly.

"But you let me think that it was them," her voice dripped with accusation.

"Yes, I did that. We have always wanted you to go after them, and this helped us reach that goal. I'm not proud of that. But I have news for you," he paused, his gaze meeting hers once more. "You're not as cold hearted as you think you are. You might be a bitch, but if you're going after them for those you care about, that means you do have feelings."

Tori chewed on her cheek for a moment, then stood, turning her back on him. "Why are you here?"

"To help you," he raised his chin in defiance. "It's not part of the plan, and Godfry is going to be pissed off when he finds out that Mason and I have chosen to join you. But it's ok." He glanced at the other men of her crew, "I made some bad choices where you were concerned, and I don't want this to be another one. That's why I wanted you to know you're friends are safe, more or less. They aren't being hunted as far as we know."

"Thanks," her voice had grown soft, her eyes on the water. She sighed, aware that they had taken the conversation as far as they could at that point. "Go inside and get yourself cleaned up. There's only one bedroom left, so you two will have to share. And you can borrow some clothes out of Danny's closet. I think they will more or less fit you, and he has a ton."

Eli rose without argument, and Mason watched him go while grinding his teeth. "You believe him?" he asked quietly, when he was out of earshot.

Tori nodded, "Yeah," and left it at that.

"He was right about Godfry. As soon as he learns about this, things are going to get ugly."

"I know. And you told me that you think Godfry's behind all of this. That things were happening that he had a hand in," she waited for his affirmative gesture. "Do you think he's actually working for them?"

"I have been unable to make any concrete connections," he replied calmly. "But I don't think he is providing them with information, at any rate. If he were, there wouldn't have been anything to gain by torturing Doug."

"Right," Michael agreed. "We still have a lot of details to work out."

"No, we don't," Brett countered evenly. "We need t' keep our eye on th' prize. If she wants t' put an end t' their reign, then that's th' only details we need; how t' get t' them."

Tori pursed her lips, "I think so too; we need to narrow our objective. I say we find out where they hide and go straight for the heart."

"After we eliminate the Spiders," Brett half-heartedly agreed.

"The Spiders," she repeated. "So they really do exist."

"Oh yeah, they exist," he offered, "After th' Dragons had disappeared, they had us teaming up with them a few times. Right nasty bunch o' guys, too. Suffice it t' say, we take out them, then cut off the head o' th' snake, an' eliminate as many o' them as we can." He glared at Mason, "Unless you was thinkin' you'd arrest 'em all."

"No," the tallest man in the group replied. "This is all off the books, and we will not be prosecuting any of these bastards if all goes well. And the only person who would be upset about that is Warren La Buff, not that I care what he thinks."

"You have your other clothes with you?" Tori glanced up and down his tall frame. "You need to fit in with the group, you know."

"Yeah," he relaxed his stance. "I do, and I'll change if you like."

Michael clenched his jaw at the man's tone when he spoke to the girl. "Go change, then, and we can get started forming our plans," he directed. He knew at the moment, she was still his, but glancing around at the others, he had to admit, the odds weren't good that she would be by the end.

We Need a Plan

While Eli dug through Brian's closet and drawers, searching for more suitable clothing, Mason returned to the car to retrieve his bag of biker gear. Sliding into the driver's seat to move the car closer to the house, he chuckled to himself. *Damn she was hot the last time I wore that get-up.* He grimaced, the thought of his hand beneath her leather skirt causing a stiffness in his groin. *Shit. Keep your mind on the job,* he commanded to himself, *and you'll increase your odds of surviving this mess tremendously.*

The rest of his new team was still gathered in the living area when he re-entered the house and made his way up the stairs. Finding Eli in their quarters, he tossed their bags on the bed. "You ok?"

"Yes," Eli rolled up the sleeves on the button down shirt. "I hope she didn't intend for me to wear those tee shirts with the disgusting pictures on the front." Bending over, he put two rolls on each leg of his jeans and slipped on the shoes.

"I'm sure you're fine for the time being." Hunt studied the other man for a moment, "Hey, listen. I want you to know that I'm sorry. I think I misjudged you."

"Why is that?" Eli didn't bother to look up.

"Because you said the two of you didn't really have anything in common. I always wondered why you let things go as far as you did. That's how it is though, when you've got the hots for someone. You start thinking with the wrong

33

part of your anatomy." He was nodding, well aware how easy it would be to fall into that trap, especially when a girl like Tori was involved.

Eli breathed deeply and allowed the air to escape slowly before he met the taller man's gaze. "It was more than that. I know other people don't understand. Probably because I have forced myself to do my job, despite what my heart was telling me. At least my head is clear enough I can see that she and I are from different worlds, and any life we might have ever had together would never be right."

"Wow," his counterpart breathed. "So you're willing to throw away your career; maybe even your life, for some girl you know will never be yours?"

"She's mine in here," he patted his chest with the flat of his palm. "That's enough for me." He stood, inspecting the sneakers with a disgusted grunt, "Two sizes too big. Oh, well. Let's go find out if there's anything to eat around here."

Brunch was being served when the two men entered the dining room. Seated at the head of the glass table, Tori felt a little odd as she surveyed the men who formed a circle before her. Enrique and then Brett to her left, her mate and then Eli to her right, Mason on the far end. Nodding to herself, she had the strong feeling that they were missing someone.

Shaking off the odd premonition, she was eager to get started. "We need to gather our resources. Start compiling what we know about The Organization, as well as the Spiders. After that, we can begin to decide what to do with it."

Reaching into his pocket between bites, Mason withdrew his ring of keys, tossing them out into the center of the table. "Those will get us into the offices in Chicago," he breathed calmly. "But we will need a computer to access the files on the flash drives."

"You made copies of the files?" Eli stared at him

incredulously. "They're encrypted, aren't they?"

"Yes," Mason agreed with a nod. "I made copies of everything that was within my clearance, so once we have a computer we will be able to open them using my access codes. However, you and I both know that Godfry kept many of the files on paper only, in folders in his office."

"Old school," Eli agreed. "Everyone made fun of him about that behind his back. Said it was time for him to retire, if he couldn't get with the program."

"I'm sure that's not why he did it," Tori interrupted their conversation. "It was to keep the information safe." She was shoving the food around on her plate, not really eating enough to make a dent.

"Is something wrong with your lunch?" Michael's eyes narrowed.

"I'm not very hungry," she lifted her glass to gulp her water, hoping it would wash away the nausea so she could finish her meal.

Still watching her, her mate agreed calmly, "I think you're right. I'm sure if he's dirty, keeping his files hidden would be a priority. That means we need to get a look at them." He pointed his fork at the two agents, "Too bad you already called them in. They may have been able to get a peek, but I'm sure they will be locked out completely within a matter of hours."

"Why?" Eli countered. "No one knows that we have crossed over, at least not yet."

"How long will it take before that happens?" Tori inquired, managing a few bites.

"Hard to say," Mason supplied. "If we want anything out of the Chicago office, we should go after it soon, and hope we can get it before it does."

"We need rides," Brett took the opportunity to speak up. "We can't keep flyin' all over th' place. Makes us far too easy t' track. An' we're not all gonna fit in their little Mazda, neither."

"Agreed," Michael chewed quickly. "We need to pick up a set of bikes and head towards the Windy City, and Eli can follow along in their car like they are still tailing us. Do you check in with Godfry?"

"When anything happens or changes, yes," Eli nodded. "Actually, I think that might work. Of course, when we get there, things will get more complicated. I have no idea where we can hang out that won't draw attention."

"I knows a place," Enrique called out loudly, causing the others to stare. "Sorry, got a little excited," he grinned recalling the last night he had spent inside the cabin, Tori in his arms as they slept. "It's out of the way, and no one'll bother us there."

Brett flicked his gaze between the woman at the far end of the table and the two men who flanked her. "Yeah, tha's a good place," he concurred easily. "We'll take the car this afternoon and pick out some bikes. Be on the road tonight if we're lucky, or first thing in the morning at the latest."

Looking around at the group of men, Tori dropped her gaze to the ring of keys. "You guys can go straight to Chicago. I have to make a stop along the way, but I'll meet you there."

Michael's face popped up from his meal to stare at her. "You're not riding behind me?"

"No," she avoided looking at him. "I want my own bike. Like I said, there's something I need to do, so you and the rest of these guys go on, and I'll catch up to you."

The air became thick, as the group could see the tension between the husband and wife. Pushing his plate back, Michael folded his hands in front of his face, "Baby girl, I don't think that's a good idea. I think we need to stick together."

AVENGED

Unexpectedly, Tori slapped the table with an open palm, half leaping to her feet. "I don't give a fuck what you think is or isn't a good idea! I'm in charge here; you got that?" she stabbed herself in the chest with a finger as she berated him. "Get the bikes and let's get the hell out of here," she called over her shoulder as she stormed out of the room.

Out of the Past

Stomping up the stairs, Tori fumed to herself. *I can't believe him. I thought Eddie was a controlling son of a bitch; at least he was up front about it.* Inside their quarters, she made her way over to the wide expanse of glass that overlooked the lake.

Her mind turning, she recalled the way that she and Eddie had played their game; how she had always pretended that she wanted him and enjoyed being his woman. *I slit that bastard's throat when I finally had the chance.* Leaning against the window, she placed her arms above her head and heaved a heavy sigh.

If he thinks he can control me, he's got another thing coming. The two of them had never had a physical altercation. She had sparred with Eddie many times as her instructor, as well as taking his beatings when he was pissed. However, Michael had refrained from ever raising a hand to her.

Unexpectedly, her mood changed, and a tear streaked down her cheek. It hung on the edge of her jaw before she pulled her hand down to wipe it away. *You sure blubber a lot lately,* she admonished herself; there had been a time you couldn't make her cry, no matter how badly you beat her. *Did Michael do this to me? Make me all soft and weak?*

He was never heavy-handed with his wife, treating her with the utmost respect. The few times he had ever been aggressive with her, she could count on one hand. She chuckled, recalling the hot sex he had given her the day she had strutted about for the neighbors in her white string bikini. *God, I love that man.*

Pulling herself together, Tori made her way into the bathroom to repair her makeup. Digging in her bag, she pushed the pack of pads aside, grasping her container of pills to take the third placebo. She hadn't started yet and opted to carry a pad instead of wearing it as there was no sense in wasting them until it came.

Primping complete, Tori made her way back downstairs, promising herself she was going to hold her temper in check. "We ready to go shopping?" she inquired, observing the somber expressions their faces held.

"Yes," Michael agreed. "You and I will take a cab, and the rest of the guys will ride over in the car. We've located a dealership that has new and used, so we'll have a huge selection to choose from, and we have plenty of cash to make the purchases," he indicated the stacks of money on the piano, divided into equal portions so they each would have a share.

"That sounds like a plan," she agreed with a small smile. "We should take all of our stuff, too. Leave from there and head north."

"Get it together then, and I'll call a cab. We'll meet out front," he swung his gaze around the others, who were obediently moving to retrieve their gear.

Half an hour later, Tori and Michael slid into the back of the taxi. Watching the rest of her crew climb into the small grey, four-door sedan, she felt a stab of loneliness, surrounded by her favorite men, and yet alone in her world. Pushing at her bag that rested against her leg, she nestled into the seat, the car rolling towards the familiar life of men and motorcycles she had always known.

Arriving at the dealership, the group spread out, each moving between the rows of machines in search of the one that called to them. Her hand sliding across the leather seat of an older model, Tori's heart began to race. Fingers beginning to tremble, she knelt down next to the engine and touched the shiny metal, *right year... right make and model. It's not his, but damn it's close.* "I'll take this one," she called out over her shoulder.

"Wouldn't you like to give it a test ride?" the salesmen asked in a warm voice.

"That won't be necessary," she replied crisply, lifting her pack onto her shoulder. She was prepared to spend her entire portion of the money if she had to, and whatever issues her new ride had, she would repair. "Who do I pay?"

"Right this way," he waved his hand to indicate his cubical in the back of the showroom. "We can get started on the paperwork. That's an older model, but I think we can still get financing with the right amount of down payment."

"I have cash," she replied calmly. "Ring it up, and I'm good to go," she smiled at the thought of owning a bike, *just like Eddie's.*

A few minutes later, the transaction was complete, and she rolled her new toy out front. Kicking it over eagerly, she grinned at the way that it purred; *someone really loved this old thing.* Revving the engine, she was overcome with the urge to fly. Securing her pack in the saddlebag, she twirled her hair and pulled it inside her jacket, leaning forward as the bike built up speed when she rolled away.

Returning to the shop a short time later, she discovered that the remainder of the group had also found what they were looking for. Smiling, she noticed that Mason Hunt appeared to be at ease with his new ride and sporting the familiar uniform. "Nice choice," she called to him playfully, her mind turning to what he would look like without the jacket and jeans covering his magnificent body.

"Thanks," he responded coolly. Eyeing hers, he grinned, "That's not too much for you? I mean, it's not what I imagined."

"I like 'em big," she tossed back, an unmistakable vibe bouncing between the pair. "If we're set, we should get moving." She felt a little out of breath, her mind leaping to what would happen when the group stopped for the night, and the dark closed in around them. Stealing a glance at her husband, she noticed he was keeping his eyes on his work.

"Hey, Mike," she called to him, "You sure you can take this? Not too late to back out."

"Nope," he kept his gaze fixed on his gear, his hands finishing securing the load, "I'm fine. Do what you gotta do." He shot her a quick glance, refusing to make a scene over what lay ahead of them.

Twisting the throttle, she caused the bike to roar loudly. Sneering as she surveyed the group one last time, she waited for them to mount up and follow her as she rolled off the lot, and out onto the highway.

Dirty Boys

Out on the open road, Tori began to relax into her old self. She had never ridden on her own as a rule but was quite comfortable controlling the oversized machine. Her shades protecting her eyes from the glare, she looked the men over each time that they pulled in for gas or a break, sizing them up and trying to decide which one she would like to fuck first. *You know you're going to,* she teased herself with an elated grin.

Of course, she had already had them all. *All but Mason, that is. I may have to do a bit of work, to convince him to fall in line.* The sun was sinking low in the sky as she began to search for a place they could crash for the night. *I wonder if he's a dirty boy,* she pondered as they parked next to a picnic table at a roadside rest stop. The area was nestled into a tree line, and mostly hidden from the road; *perfect for nasty entertainment.*

Nodding her approval at the location, the men began setting up camp. *If he's not,* she finalized her plan for the newest member of her crew, *at least I know I can count on Enrique; he always wants to get nasty.* She fingered a tube of gel in her pocket, anticipating the fulfillment of her desires.

Building a fire, the group grilled the steaks they had picked up in the last town, the conversation at a minimum as the tension began to build. Tori made sure she stayed close to her primary target, unable to wipe the eager smile from her

42

lips while she made small talk. "So, Mason, how long have you been a biker?"

"I'm not, really," he chuckled, "Part of the job, I guess. I did some time studying about the culture, preparing for a sting operation I was involved in a few years ago." He cut his eyes over at her, noticing that she had stripped down to a muscle shirt, her breasts clearly defined through the thin material.

"So, were you ever inducted?" she panted, leaning over against his bike as he squatted down next to it, putting her cleavage in his face.

Switching to Russian, he spoke softly, "We are going to stick to business, Tori."

Her mouth fell open, her surprise tumbling out as she gaped at him. "What kind of business?" she managed in kind, aware that her husband also spoke the tongue, and the conversation was not completely private.

"I'm not going to fuck you," he stated flatly. Standing abruptly, he towered over her, taking her breath away. "You see that man over there, pretending like he doesn't care?" he indicated her mate with a short nod.

Not bothering to look, lines began to form in her features as she stood as well, the bike between them. "Yeah, I see him. So what? He knew what it was going to be like when we got here."

"No," her prey shook his head. "That's not what this is. That's not what this is about." He reached up, allowing himself to toy with her hair, his voice dropping to a low, gravely rumble, "I can't say that I don't want to. You are damn sure good at pushing the buttons." His gaze dropped, staring at the heaving mounds, the pink rose rising and falling perfectly.

"If you want it, you should hit up Enrique. He's got no morals, and I'm sure he would be more than happy to shove you over the table and pound the hell out of you. Brett might be as well, but I don't think you want him as badly." He grinned at the frown that tugged at her lips, aware that he clearly had the upper hand, "Otherwise, I guess you could always see if your husband would be willing to oblige."

"Did you forget about Eli?" she scoffed, "He's here too, you know."

"Eli isn't going to touch you," he leaned in closer, his voice lower still. "He's in love with you, and the last thing he would ever do, is fuck you in front of everyone. I'm not even sure that Michael would. Something about respect. Something you failed to learn in that messed up world you came from."

Tori's hand shot up, slapping him smoothly across the face. "What the fuck do you know about it?" she demanded loudly, bringing the exchange back in English. "You don't know a God damned thing!" She was shouting, everyone staring at the two of them.

Raising his hand calmly, Mason massaged his wounded jaw, "I know that you're still that girl, lost back there, somewhere; searching for who you really are. I'm not going to touch you," he announced loudly, also in English. "And any man here with a sense of dignity won't touch you either."

Turning his back on her, he grabbed his bedroll and walked away. Her chest still heaving, Tori was overcome with the urge to throw a tantrum; if only there were something at hand she could smash. Pushing her hands against her face and up into her hair, she lifted the long dark strands, pulling them tightly so that her features became distorted, and her scalp tingled.

Releasing her grip, she called out, "Is that how it is? Everyone's going to leave me hanging?" For the first time in her life, she realized the true disadvantage of *not* being a man. She could want to have them, but in the end, there had to be a certain degree of cooperation on their part, or she wasn't going to get her way. "You guys suck, you know that!?!"

Michael moved over to her, his arms sliding around her and pulling her against him firmly. Squeezing as hard as he dared, he breathed into the mass of dark curls, "You're going to be fine. It's a drug; like any other."

Allowing him to hold her, she fumed in a scathing torrent, "I hate you! I don't know why I married you. That's why they won't. Because of this stupid ring. Because of you!" She expected her words to drive him away, some sick plot in the back of her mind that they could break up, and then Mason would take her.

Michael only squeezed her tighter. "Yup. Funny how things sometimes work."

Struggling to free herself, Tori grabbed her bedroll and headed down the road, ready to sleep away from the group that had disappointed her. Stopping in front of Enrique, she looked him in the eye, "You coming?" He wasn't her first choice, but he would do.

His eyes darted around at the other men, and he shoved his hands in his pockets. *Fuck me. They think I'm banging her as it is.* He had never cared what others thought about him, and never thought he would turn down the chance to be with her; she was his addiction, plain and simple. Pursing his lips, he knew he wasn't the one she really wanted, and he needed to be wanted. "Naw, I'm not gonna be your last resort."

"Fine!" she tossed her chin into the air, "I'll sleep alone." She marched down the path, dropping onto the ground and leaning against a small tree a few hundred yards from their camp.

To her surprise, her mate arrived next to her, carrying his

own pack a few minutes later. "What the fuck are you doing?" she demanded as he began to unroll his sleeping bag.

"Getting ready for bed," he replied calmly without looking up. He spread his bag flat, creating the bottom of a double sized bed. Reaching for hers, he unrolled it and began to smooth it out over his, to form the top.

"I'm not sleeping with you!" she spit curtly.

"Yes, you are," he lifted his face to stare at her, on all fours in front of her. "You're my wife, and you're going to do your part." Turning to sit, he removed his boots, then moved to his belt, "Get your clothes off, and let's get on with it."

Tori stared at him, mouth open wide as she struggled to breath, "You're not serious."

"The fuck if I'm not," he hoisted his shirt over his head, "You're not the only one who's different out here. I told you; I'm not the nice guy you think I am."

Tori didn't move; her thoughts swirling. *He's putting on a show. He wants the rest of the guys to think he's tough.* Slowing her breathing, she struggled to bring her heart rate under control, "All right, I can play along."

"This isn't a game," he was down to his white cotton briefs when he turned, reaching for her. Tori stiffened against the bark behind her, his hands gripping her muscled biceps and pulling her onto the makeshift bed.

"Kick your boots off," he commanded.

She lay on her back, staring up at him, her pulse in her throat as she struggled to comply. "Please don't do this," her bottom lip began to quiver as soon as the cool air reached her feet through her socks.

"Do what?" he demanded with a growl, "I'm going to fuck you. That's what you wanted. You made it quite clear you were in the mood, offering yourself to everyone in the whole fucking crew!"

Removing her jacket, he reached into the pocket, tossing her tube on the corner of their mat and the leather aside, "What?" he eyed her startled expression, "You thought I didn't see you take it?" Grabbing the button on her jeans, he freed them and began yanking them down her legs.

Tori didn't argue, allowing him to remove the denim and lift her shirt over her head. She felt no tenderness in his touch as he unhooked her bra and removed her panties in an equally brusque fashion. Flipping her over onto her belly, he pulled her onto her knees, so that her rear end was at a more comfortable height, and pushed himself into her warm hollow.

"See? Dripping wet. Filthy whore," he berated her as he smacked against her. He grasped a hand full of her dark locks and pulled her back against himself more firmly. "You want to hate me; I'll give you something to hate me for."

Grasping the blanket tightly, she suppressed the urge to cry out, the feel of him inside her driving her mad. Her mind stuck in Florida, on the first time he had taken her like this, she recalled how good he was when he fucked her angry. Her pulse quickened as she realized she wanted more. "My God, baby, please don't stop," she breathed into the cloth before calling out, "Hurry up. We need to get some sleep…"

Catching her hair next to her scalp, he pulled her head back, "Shut up! I'll take all God damn night if I want." He nuzzled her ear through her ebony locks. Biting at it, he could feel her tremble beneath him. Sliding his hand from her hip, across her belly to squeeze her breast, he moaned. "I don't know if I can do the rest… I thought I could, but…" he sobbed slightly, his grip on her hair relaxing a bit.

"It's ok, love," she breathed, "Do what you like." She placed her hand over the back of his, squeezing herself with his hand, "You feel so good, baby… please don't stop."

He grinned at her praise; his strength renewed. Sliding

his hand down her smooth skin, he gripped her fur covered mound, pressing it against the bone beneath it. Sliding in and out of her with firm stabs, he drove her as hard as he could, listening to her cries grow louder and aware that the rest of the group could more than likely hear them.

Continuing his assault on her wet folds, he could feel the sweat forming over her silky flesh, the cool air of the night around them. His knees growing tired, he wasn't ready to finish, and pushed himself in deeper to rest, panting into the back of her head once more. "Jesus Christ," he begged, "Rollover and get on top."

Pushing him out of her, she was more than willing to comply. "Lay down," she commanded, ready to take the upper hand.

Throwing her leg over him, as if he were a fine leather seat, she pushed herself down upon him and ran her fingers through the hairs that hid her name. An unexplainable joy tingled her flesh as the waves of ecstasy washed over her a moment later, and she could feel the weakness sap her strength as she called his name into the darkness.

Tugging at her mane as it cascaded down her back and over his hand, he allowed his own release within her, his groans equal to hers in strength and volume. "My God, you're killing me," he breathed into the dimple of her neck when she stretched out across him, her heart pounding against his.

Laying over him, she ignored the comment, focused on the inhale and exhale that caused her nostrils to flare. Her fingers crept up the side of his face to grasp his golden curls and tug at them firmly, and then relax as her strength slowly returned. "You're a real asshole, you know that," she teased.

"Yeah, I am," his white teeth flashed in the dim light. "And you're my bitch. Don't ever fucking forget it."

Back to Chicago

Tori awoke the following morning to find the sky was shifting into the fuzzy gray of early dawn. She was vaguely aware of her husband's body pressed firmly against hers, the weight of his left leg holding her down as it draped across her. Reaching up, she traced the line of his left arm that dangled on her chest, her fingertips moving daintily through the hairs to massage it.

A faint smile curled her lips, the peace she felt within her unmatched in weeks. *He wasn't able to go all the way,* she mused, *but he damn sure got close enough.* Her mind sifting through their rough encounter, she realized, *he won't ever be as wild as I am,* and she would never be as tame as him. But the parts where they overlapped were perfect.

She could feel him shifting slightly, her caress bringing him into the realm of consciousness. She shuddered as a soft *hi* filtered through her hair to reach her ear. Sliding her fingers along the appendage until they found the end, she wove her fingers with his, a deep sigh escaping her lungs; "Hi."

He grinned, pushing himself up onto his elbow while maintaining his claim on her body, hand sliding down her front to rest on her belly between her navel and her pubic bone. "You feel better, I take it?"

"Yes," she exhaled again, "I don't see how you do it." Her fingers encircled his once more, and he returned his palm to her breast. "What would you have done, if one or more of them had given in to me?" she asked, tilting her head enough to see his outline against the glow of the sky above them.

"I told you not to worry about that, didn't I?" he smiled, no hint of anger in his voice. "You do what you need to do, and be who you need to be. Don't worry about whether or not I'm going to judge you."

"You know that doesn't make sense," she offered. "I told you before; men don't let their wives fuck other men. Not if they can help it."

Ignoring the comment, he explored the line of her jaw, his digits finding their way into her hair before he leaned over to kiss her. As soon as their lips touched, he grew stiff. Ready to take her, he pushed himself up, grabbing her legs and making his way between them, she moaning at his assertiveness.

"I trust you," he nuzzled her face, "Or maybe I like the thought of you being with them. I'm not sure which, and you can take your pick." He folded her legs and drove himself against her full force.

It only took a few minutes before he quivered from his release. She lay flat onto their bedding, wrapping her arms around him to prevent his getting up. "You said I was your bitch."

"You are my bitch," he poked his name. "But you did the marking for yourself." He grinned at her squinty face and laughed, "What? It's the truth."

"I need you to take the rest of the group on to Chicago today. There really is something I have to do." She played with his curls, waiting for him to respond.

Pushing himself up, he sat back on his heels. Staring down at her naked splendor, her skin unmarked in the light of daybreak, he agreed, "Ok, I can do that. The guys know where we're going, that cabin they talked about."

"Yes, I'll meet you there in a day or two."

He didn't want to move, returning his hand to her belly for a brief moment. "Be careful, ok?"

"I'm always careful," she grinned, catching him and pulling him down to her for another kiss. "I love you."

"You love me, huh?" he chuckled. "Someday you're going to make up your mind." Pushing himself up, he stood, looking around for his clothes. Dressing quickly, the pair rolled up their bags and returned to find the rest of the group still slumbering.

Situating her gear, she turned to her mate, "I'm going to head out. You can wake them and be on your way." Standing next to him, she was overcome with regret, an odd feeling that something dark lay in their future. "You know that I meant that, don't you?"

"I know," he looped his arm around her, pulling her tight against him, "And we have a lot to discuss, you and I. But now is not the time. We have work to do. So get out of here." Slapping her on the rear, he kissed the tip of her nose.

Kicking her leg over her ride, she flickered a brief smile and then she was gone.

Watching her grow smaller in the distance, Michael slid his hand across his chest. Finding the spot he knew held her name, he pressed his palm flat against it, a deep sigh escaping him noisily.

"Well, I guess you two had a good night," Mason called out to him, rolling over to get up from his sack.

"Yeah," Michael agreed absently, pulling his eyes away from the road, "We're supposed to meet her at the cabin in Chicago in a few days." Glancing around, he could see that everyone was awake. "Where's Eli?"

"In the car," Enrique laughed, tugging his shirt over his head. "What a pussy, can't even sleeps on the ground."

"You're kidding me," Michael glared over at the vehicle,

then strolled over to pound on the glass, "Hey, time to get up, princess."

Eli sat up from his curled position in the back seat, waving at the other man. Slipping on his shoes, he climbed out, "I don't suppose we have any coffee." He stretched in an exaggerated fashion, his joints popping as he moved.

"No," Brett informed him flatly. "However, we'll pull in at th' first diner we see so we can have that an' some food. We're gonna ride hard, so we can get t' th' cabin an' get set up."

"Great," Eli muttered. "I never liked camping when I was a kid, so I can tell riding around with you lot is going to be a real blast."

Michael laughed out loud, muttering the word *camping* under his breath. It only took a few minutes for them to stow their gear.

Michael and Brett exchanged stares a few times as they moved, the older man somewhat bothered that she had chosen to give her orders to her husband and not himself. Climbing onto his bike, he knew they would have to decide who was, in fact, her second, one way, or another.

You're the Man

Tori followed the same route she knew the guys would take; but traveling alone, she made much better time. Eventually cutting across to St. Louis, she decided she needed to make the call. Spotting a payphone outside of a convenience store shortly before dark, she went inside to get a roll of quarters and returned to the device.

Reaching for her wallet, she pulled out the small card that Geek had presented to her the night they brought justice to the Scorpions; the same night that Debra Paisley had been murdered. Pushing her sorrow aside, Tori dropped in the coins and punched the buttons to complete the connection. After a few rings, a woman's voice picked up the line.

Quickly, Tori asked to speak to Kevin, becoming surprised at the other female's resistance. "Kevin doesn't live here," she replied abruptly. "May I ask who's calling?"

Perplexed, Tori hesitated a moment before deciding to proceed with her plan, "I'm sorry, I realize it's probably late. I'm an old friend of his, and I'm going to be passing through Kansas tomorrow. I was hoping he might meet me for lunch. Or dinner. Whenever he might be free."

"I see," the voice replied, "But you still haven't given me your name."

Grasping the headset tighter, her hand slid down the metal rings of the cord, *Jesus woman, just tell me how to find him.* "My name is Tori," she breathed softly into the device.

"Tori! Oh my God!" her tone became shrill, clearly having heard of the girl. "Here's his number. Be sure to call him right away. He works nights and will be leaving any minute, and you'll miss him if you don't."

Thanking her, the girl quickly ended the call and hung up, eager to dial the new extension. A moment later, she could hear the young man's voice on the other end as it bade her hello. "Hello, Geek," she replied softly.

"Holy shit! Is that you?"

"Who else's gonna call ya Geek?" she mocked him with a flicker of southern. "I need to see you if you don't mind. It's urgent." She didn't dare discuss business over the phone, and knew her best chance of persuading him to help would be in person.

"Yeah, I understand," his words hinted of eagerness. "When and where?"

"I'm in St. Louis," she explained. "I decided to call rather than showing up at your mom's house unannounced."

"Well, it's a damn good thing," he replied crisply. "'Cause I'm not in Kansas anymore."

Tori could feel the air catch in her lungs, *son of a bitch*. It never occurred to her that he might have moved. "Jesus Christ. So, where are you?"

"I'm in Springfield, Illinois. Actually, I'm going to school here, at the Midwest Technical Institute," he supplied with obvious pride.

"Never heard of it," she almost shouted with relief. "But at least you're not too far away. How do I get there?"

"Take fifty-five and it'll bring you straight into town. There's a coffee shop on the corner of Peoria and Garfield. I'll meet you there at six-thirty when I get off work."

"Thanks, Geek," she smiled to herself, "How long will it take me to get there? I need to get some sleep if I can."

"It's about a two hour trip," he advised, "And don't

worry. If you're late, I'll wait for you."

"Thanks, Geek," she breathed a second time. Hanging up, she trotted over to her bike, ready for a hotel, a hot shower and a nap before she made her way to meet him.

Her check in went smoothly, and she lugged her bag into her room. Dropping it on the bed, she kicked off her clothes and unleashed the spray of the shower, moaning as the warm cascade splashed across her body. Washing her hair and tired frame, she remained in the tub when she was finished.

Placing her forehead against the plastic coated wall, she enjoyed the feel of the water running down her back. Lifting her hand, she stared at her silver ring, her mind returning to her mate. Her thoughts had scarcely been of little else during her ride, even though she had repeatedly tried to redirect them to the matter at hand.

You really don't love him enough; she allowed herself to ponder for a moment. Reaching to cut off the water, she wrapped herself in the towel, recalling the time she had spent with her brother at the diner in Texas, and had confided in him that she never had actual feelings of her own. *I borrowed them;* she confessed to herself, dropping the cloth on the floor and rummaging in her bag.

I know he didn't understand. No one really did, and she had been turning the idea in her mind. *I felt like a mirror, only capable of reflecting. Whatever emotion I was given, I returned. No more, no less.* The only real emotion she could claim was anger, and it was still the one she felt the strongest.

Flicking off the light, she slid between the sheets, the exhaustion taking its toll. She groggily considered Enrique, and some of the others, and the emotions that passed between them. *I'm not reflecting anymore.* Closing her eyes, she focused on clearing her mind, a sadness settling over her. "I can't let anything happen to any of them; I love them too much," she whispered into the darkness.

It had been years since she had entertained such an idea that she was capable of real emotion. *I have so much at stake here; so much to lose.* She often claimed to care about people, but now she could *feel* it, like a heavy rock resting on her chest. Breathing deeply, she realized that her defenses had been broken and that her husband was at the top of a very long list; her genuine concern for so many could no longer be ignored.

The following morning, Geek sat patiently, already in a booth when she arrived at the diner, and she made her apologies as she slid into the seat across from him. "Thank you so much for waiting for me."

"Of course," he smiled. "I have to admit; I wasn't surprised to get your call. I guess you could say, I've been looking forward to it."

Tori looked up at the waitress, "Water, and dry toast, please."

"Dry toast?" her friend teased, "What the hell kinda breakfast is that?"

"The only one I can keep down," she replied, sliding her jacket off and fanning herself, "Isn't it hot in here to you?"

"Why can't you eat breakfast?" he inquired smoothly.

"I don't know," she sipped her glass of ice water. "I picked up a bug a couple of weeks ago, and I can't seem to shake it. I get sick whenever I eat certain things, and breakfast is one of them."

"I see," he glared at her, refusing to voice his thoughts aloud. Deciding to let it go, he inquired with a grin, "So, what brings you here?"

"Well, you know, we never did finish off the powers that be," she replied calmly, picking up the toast to tear it apart.

"Fuck me, we're going after them?" his preparedness was apparent.

"Wow, I was fairly certain I would have to convince you to help," she flicked her eyes up at him in surprise.

"Yeah, pretty crazy, huh. But, after I got home, and started evaluating my life, I realized it was entirely my fault they were able to trap me to begin with. I never appreciated what I had, and I've been working on that," he nodded for affect. "That's one reason I've gone back to school; to prepare myself for a better future."

"I see," she replied calmly. "Well, I don't know anything about that. What I do know, is that I need a computer, and possibly some help cracking into some encrypted files. Not that I even know what that means exactly, and when it comes to stuff like that, you're the man for the job."

"Encrypted files," he laughed loudly. "Wow, you don't mess around. Ok, well, I need to go by my apartment and grab my gear, and we can be on our way. It's not far from here; actually, if you wanna wait here and I'll be right back. Fifteen, twenty minutes tops."

"Sure, hun. Go grab your stuff, and we'll head out." Watching him exit through the glass door, she could feel her stomach lurch. Jumping up, she bolted to the back, barely making it into the bathroom before she heaved up her dry toast with a small whimper of disgust.

What We Know

Geek returned to the diner a short time later to discover she was still sitting in the booth, her face in her hands. "You ok?" he stammered, dropping his backpack into the seat and sliding in.

"Yeah," her voice sounded weak. "I'm tired of being sick. Right this moment, what I really want is a nap."

"Didn't you sleep last night?" he glared at her. "You know, last time we joined forces, you were pretty on top of things." he grinned, recalling her past escapades. "But you ain't lookin' so hot."

"Thanks," she shot him a grin, "Let's get outta here before I have to whoop the shit outta you."

Outside, he placed his pack into her saddlebag, after some careful rearranging of her gear. "This is gonna be weird," he commented. "Isn't the girl supposed to ride in the back."

"Not when it's the bitch's bike," she tossed her curls and climbed on the front seat, securing her gloves, "You'll be fine."

The ride went smoothly, and checking her time, Tori expected to pull up at the cabin with at least a few hours before the rest of the guys got there. Instead, she and Geek arrived to find them passed out all over the place, enjoying the afternoon sun.

Locating her husband sleeping against the trunk of a tree,

she woke him with a slap on the shoulder. "Hey," she demanded, "How did you guys get here so quick?"

"We rode straight through," he grimaced, "We're beat. And we saved the bedroom in the cabin for you." He half smiled at her surprised stare.

"What about you? You're going to sleep out here on the ground with everyone else? It's fucking winter, you know," her voice was elevated, angry after the thoughts of him she had previously been considering.

"I'll stay where ever you want me to, love," he held a straight face as he replied.

"Ok, well I'm going inside to have a nap myself if you care to join me." Turning her back on him, she skipped up the few steps, treading gently on the wooden porch so as not to disturb Enrique if she could help it. *Crazy bunch of guys,* she leaned over him to find that he was still fast asleep, *why the hell didn't they get some rest? Like one day would have mattered.*

Michael watched his wife inspecting their group mate before disappearing into the cabin, opting to stay put and give her some space. Looking up into the bare branches of the tree overhead, he could see a tall skinny kid staring down at him. "Who the hell are you?" he asked pointedly.

The young man dropped onto the ground next to him, "I was about to ask you the same thing, since she didn't bother to introduce us. I'm Kevin Harris, but everyone calls me Geek." For emphasis, he offered the older man his hand.

"Well, nice to meet you... Geek, huh? Does that mean you know anything about tech stuff?" Michael noted his nod and continued, "I'm Mike, by the way, Anderson. Tori's my wife."

"Mike? As in Michael?" Geek's mind began to spin. Laughing out loud, "No shit. She said the name on her chest was 'just some guy'. Should have known that was a lie." The smile on the other man's face disappeared.

"You saw my name on her chest?" his eyes narrowed uncontrollably.

"Yeah, everyone did," Geek grew uncomfortable, holding up his hands in surrender, "Listen, I don't want in the middle of… whatever game the two of you are playing. I never touched her; all I ever did was watch, and I didn't even do that if I could help it."

"You were with the Scorpions," Michael surmised.

"Yeah, I was their tech guy," the boy brushed his hair out of his eyes. "I'd still be stuck with them, too, if Tori hadn't come along and helped me get away."

"I see. And she asked you to come help us."

"Sure did; said I was the man for the job," Geek grinned at her confidence in him. "I'm actually really good with the tech stuff, as you put it."

"Well Geek, you should find a place to sack out for a bit. We'll all get up in a couple of hours, and we can start putting together what we know." Leaning back against his spot, Michael closed his eyes to get a few more hours of shut-eye.

Standing, Geek made his way around the group, quietly inspecting them. He grinned to himself when he realized that Brett was with them as well. *Guess she didn't have the heart to take him out either.* Noting Enrique slept against the railing of the porch, he chose another spot, where the sun would warm him while he caught a bit of rest for himself.

Tori still lay passed out on the bed when Michael went to wake her and inform her that dinner was ready. Pausing next to her limp form, he lightly traced her scar with his finger, recalling that she seldom left it uncovered since she joined the band. *Must have been a rough night; or a short one.* Grasping her by the arm, he shook her gently, "Baby girl."

Her eyes in narrow slits, she whispered, "What time is it, love?"

"Almost dark," he replied softly. "Dinner's ready, if you're hungry. You haven't had much of an appetite lately, so you ought to be." His brow furrowed and he kept his voice low.

"Yeah, I'll eat," she pulled herself up to face him. "How long have I had this? Two weeks or so? I'm ready to be over it."

"Yeah," he nodded in an exaggerated fashion. "You still think you're sick?"

"Well, yeah, I'm obviously not better," she hoisted herself up, pushing past him and making her way down the narrow hall. "Did you guys save me any?" she called out loudly, while grabbing a foam plate and serving herself.

The cabin was exactly the way they had left it the last time they were there, with the sofa that faced the television, the tiny kitchen area, and the table she had used to plan the elimination of the Scorpions. Taking one of the backless stools to sit at the table, she hungrily devoured the meal, hoping she wouldn't lose it later.

"As soon as we're finished here, we need to get started with what we know," she waved her fork around at those sitting closest to her. "Brett, you and Enrique know Geek. I think you and Michael met." Geek nodded at his new acquaintance, "Did you meet Mason and Eli yet? By the way, where is Eli? I didn't see his car out front when we pulled up."

"He wanted to go home to get some of his own clothes since we were so close. He's going to get his vehicle as well, and be back out here any time now." Her heart in her throat, she stared at Mason as he spoke.

"And you guys let him run off alone? No clue if that's really where he was going?" she could hear the tremor in her voice as the level increased with every other word.

"What were we supposed t' do? Lock him up?" Brett

interceded. "You know, I wish you'd make up your mind. Either ya trust him, or ya don'."

At that moment, the door swung open, and the man in question entered the room, again wearing one of his suits and an extra-large grin.

"Hi, guys," he nodded, pausing to give the girl a small wave. "I have fantastic news. I checked in with Godfry, and told him that you had returned to Chicago, and of course left it open as, at a distance, I would have no way of knowing why."

"And that's fantastic news?" Tori bit sharply.

"No," he looked stunned for a moment. "No, the news is, they made an arrest in the fire. It seems that one of the current residents had some gang affiliations; turns out they located him somehow, and the fire was set as some form of retaliation."

"And you're sure?" Michael demanded for her.

"Yes, absolutely. There's even some security footage from a few houses down, showing the guys pulling up and exiting the vehicle carrying their cans of accelerant." He sucked in his top lip to stifle his grin, "Sorry, but I was really glad to hear that this wasn't an attack on your friends because of you."

Tori nodded, only halfheartedly able to agree. "Anything else?" she focused on keeping her tone in check.

"Well, I hope you don't mind, but I took the liberty of bringing a few extra suits for myself. You know, so I can still look official. And I've been thinking about how we can get Godfry's files." He lifted his chin towards his fellow agent, "I have a set of keys as well, but I'm pretty sure neither of us has the one to his office."

"Relax," she informed him. "If I can get inside the building, the office is a piece of cake."

"Alright, fair enough. So when are we going after them?"

Tori swung her gaze around the group, "Well, I guess we should go tonight. The sooner we get our hands on them, the better off we'll be." She held out her right hand, palm upturned towards Geek, "I brought you a computer expert. While Eli and I go and see what we can locate in Godfry's office, the rest of you can work on opening Mason's documents and plotting things out on a map."

"What things, and what map?" Mason countered.

"I dunno, a U.S. map?" she shrugged. "You realize at this point we really have no idea what we're looking for, so we don't have any way of knowing what's going to help us. That means we need to straight up brainstorm, making connections and taking notes until something stands out." Dumping the remains of her meal in the trash, she curled her fingers at the shortest man, indicating it was time for them to go.

As soon as they were out of the cabin, Mason let loose a long, low whistle, "Well, that's not good."

"What's not?" Michael scowled at the agent.

"I assumed, I guess because all the records we have indicate, that she knew a great deal about The Organization," he pursed his lips, turning the idea in his mind. "If we're starting from scratch, this could take a while."

"Relax," Brett chuckled. "This's a good group she's brought together here. Lots of us, with lots o' vantage points. It may look like scratch, but once we start piecin' together what each of us knows, I have a feelin' it's gonna snowball in a hurry."

The Buck Stops Here

Tori smiled softly, recognizing Eli's personal vehicle and climbing into the passenger seat. "You realize we'll also need access to a copy machine while we're there," she informed him as he slid in beside her.

"No, I hadn't thought of that, but you're right; we can't remove the files themselves or it will tip him off that something is up," the agent agreed.

Riding in mutual silence, Tori watched the scenery, the trees giving way to houses, followed by taller buildings. Pulling up in front of the federal office, the same one he had taken her to over a year before, she could feel her palms beginning to perspire. Looking up at the structure before she reached for the handle, her pulse quickened at the memory of everything she had shared with the group of agents, two of whom were now dead.

Coming around to her side, Eli opened the door for her, a faint smile on his lips. "Relax, it's late enough, most everyone has gone home."

"I'm fine," she countered, dragging her eyes to meet his. "I was remembering the last time you brought me here."

"Oh," he avoided her gaze, "Yeah, a long time ago. So much has happened since then." An air of sadness settled over him, causing her to hold back from entering the building.

"I really think you and I need to talk at some point. In

private, I might add," she voiced her opinion calmly.

"What's there to talk about?" he shrugged, "I don't see how rehashing the past is going to change anything."

"It doesn't have to change things," she lowered her voice, "But talking about it helps. You taught me that, and I've tried so hard to keep that in mind. It's difficult, and I appreciate what you've done for me. I'm not sure you really understand how grateful I am."

Meeting her gaze, he nodded. "I meant what I said. I don't know when I fell in love with you; I only know it hasn't gone away. We should get inside, and talk about this later." Reaching for her elbow, he guided her towards the door.

Tori stood still, glaring at the floor in front of her while Eli unlocked and relocked the glass entrance. Giving the security guard a nod, he indicated for her to follow him to the elevator. "Damn, that's lucky," he breathed when the door had closed.

Tori watched him push the button to the proper floor, "Why was that lucky?"

"He was on his phone," Eli supplied, "The doors are usually open six am to six pm. Outside of those hours, you need a key to gain access. I guess he assumes anyone that can get inside has authorization to do so."

Tori frowned at his explanation, "So if he sees us, does he report our presence to anyone?"

"Generally, no; but if anyone were to ask, I'm sure he wouldn't lie about it. But that's the thing; he didn't give us a second glance. There's no way he could describe us to anyone, or maybe even remember we were here."

Tori grinned, "I see."

The doors opening, the pair made their way down the hall to Godfry's office. Glancing up and down the narrow passage, Eli turned his back, blocking her from being in direct line of sight from the elevator, "Alright, it's your move."

Pulling out the lock pick kit, Tori selected her tools and inserted them, opening it in a matter of seconds. Moving inside, they quickly closed the door. "I'm sure that was the easy part," she lamented. Her eyes taking in the room, there stood a desk in front, and bookcases along the back wall containing drawers on the bottom half.

"No worries," he shot back smoothly. "I've seen what we're looking for. He had them at a meeting or two and out several times in between." He started opening the drawers to the enormous desk, lifting stacks of file folders and inspecting the labels. "I think they will all be together. If you see one with Doug Seeming's name on it, speak up."

Joining him in the search, Tori began rummaging through the drawers in the bookcase. A few minutes later, Eli called for her attention, "I've got something."

Lifting the stack, he pulled up a chair and took a seat, before resting the folders on his lap. Kneeling down in front of him, Tori reached out, pressing down on the tabs so she could see them for herself. Spotting the one with Doug's name on it she slid it out and flipped it open, "Jesus Christ!"

"Yes, I warned you back in LA. Whatever he knew, they got from him. Essentially... everything." He stared down at her as she sifted through the photos, sad that they were probably not as shocking to her as they would be to most people. "How much of this do you want copies of?"

"All of it," she replied flatly. "Where's the copy machine?"

"Down the hall," he supplied. "Let me take one file at a time, and copy through it, so we don't get things out of order. Less chance he will notice they've been messed with."

"Ok. While you're doing that, I'll continue to dig around, see if I find anything else that looks important." She stood, allowing him to lay the folders on the desk, before taking the top one and exiting the room. Once he had gone, she began to snoop in some of the other drawers.

Finding nothing of interest, she reached for the Rolodex on his desk, *old school.* There had been one on Brandon's desk at the halfway house, too. *With the new fancy phones, these things could become obsolete.* Glancing through the cards, she noted that it held one for Eli, as well as for Mason. Taking a second look at some of the others, she realized they could also be agents, or they could be anyone.

She jumped slightly when the door opened, eyes shooting up to find Eli's smile; "Sorry, didn't mean to startle you."

"It's ok; I'm a bit jumpy. Look what I found," she held the rack of cards out to him. "I think we should make copies of these as well."

"Oh wow, yes definitely. Here's Doug's file if you want to go through it, and I'll be back with the next one."

The pair worked their way through what turned out to be seven folders, as well as the Rolodex. Placing all of their copies into a large envelope, Tori zipped it up inside her jacket so that it would be less noticeable when they left. Eli placed the files back into the drawer as he had found them, and they closed the door behind them.

Ten minutes later, they were back inside the car, relieved that the security guard had been too busy pressing buttons on his device to even look up when they passed in front of his counter. "He isn't worth much," Eli commented once they were outside of the building.

"Thank God for that," Tori grinned at the man beside her. "I think we got some good information though. I can't wait to see what Geek can come up with on the phone numbers."

"He knows how to track people, and use the GPS system?" Eli inquired as he started the engine.

"Yes, he does, and how to get personal information," she

replied into the darkness. "You know about that stuff?"

"Of course," he replied with a soft laugh, "A very useful tool in my line of work." He hesitated, drawing a deep breath before diving in, "I guess Enrique probably told you about some of my more... unfortunate choices."

"You mean the fact that you sent him to kill Michael," she bit her words, suppressing her anger. "I've tried not to think about that since all it does is piss me off."

"Understandably so. However, I have to admit, that was back when I was still under the delusion that you and I could have had a future together," he adjusted his grip on the wheel. "I really am sorry, as well as glad he didn't carry out my plan. I know Mike is very good for you."

Tori's jaw dropped, surprised that he would think so. "Did Godfry tell you to do that? I thought he was in charge."

"He is," Eli shrugged. "He set up the committee and delegated the jobs to us. You were my job. While you were in the hospital, it was my responsibility to make you comfortable and draw out what you knew. Then, after you were moved to LA, my focus was shifted. Enrique was the foothold we were going to use to get to the Scorpions, but it didn't work."

"He didn't cooperate," she concluded for him.

"No, and no amount of persuasion that I was able to give him helped. I only asked him to kill your husband out of jealousy. I truly am sorry," his eyes flicked over at her, then back to the road. "One of the files we copied tonight was part of my research as well. Some things that Godfry had me looking for. I had no idea at the time, but as I was making the copies, I think I figured out why."

Tori frowned, "I guess you can tell me about it when we get to the cabin, so that everyone else can hear, too. I wanted to talk to you about something personal while we have the chance."

She could hear his exaggerated inhale across the dark interior. Swinging her gaze to look out the glass to her right, she noted they were already on the outside edges of town, and she would have to hurry if she were going to have her say.

"I need to apologize to you," she kept her focus on the dried greenery flashing by in the shadows. "I shouldn't have pushed you to have sex with me. I should have known better."

"How would you have known better?" he demanded. "You know, I realize you want to talk about this, but there really isn't much to say. You grew up in a very different world. You didn't understand, and you're not the one that is to blame. I am."

She chewed the inside of her cheek, not wanting to argue with him as he went on.

"I want you to have a happy life, Tori. I would have loved, and on some levels would still like, for you to be my girl. But you're not. You're not even close, and after being reunited as we have been…" he paused, shifting in his seat as they made the last turn, "It would never have been right. I have very strong feelings for you, but there's no real foundation for them. For us. We have very different lives; we are very different people. And no amount of wishful thinking is ever going to change that." He reached up, shutting off the engine, allowing his hands to fold into his lap.

"I appreciate what you did for me. Then, and now," she managed quietly. She still did not look at him, her sadness engulfing her, causing her to feel weary. Grabbing the knob, she felt the sudden urge to breathe fresh air as if she were suffocating inside the cramped space. She wasn't sure what she had expected him to say, or where she thought the conversation would lead, but that certainly wasn't it, and all she wanted to do at the moment was to get away.

Devil's Advocate

Tori entered the cabin to discover the group had taken her advice, at least in part. Pulling the envelope out of her jacket, she laid it on the counter, turning to look over their map. "So, what're the markings?" she pondered aloud.

"We opened up all of the electronic files and began laying out the focal points of the documents if there were any." Geek took over the briefing, grabbing his computer to show her the screen, "And we needed some confirmation on a few of the details from you. Oh, and I wanted you to explain this to me." He lay a page on the table; a large daisy drawn in the center of it.

"Oh my God," she gasped, smiling to see that Eli had joined them, "You remember the first time I showed you this?"

"Yes, very vividly," he replied. "You also shared it with the committee. What's it doing here?"

"There was a description of it in some of the documents we were able to access, as well as your reports from the hospital when you were visiting her," Mason supplied.

Tori reached for the page, her gaze fluttering nervously at Brett for a moment, "I divulged a bit more than I implied. But I guess you've already figured that out."

"Yeah, baby girl." He pulled his arms across his chest, refusing to come down on her. "What's done is done. All we can do now is hope that we can get t' th' source."

"The source," she repeated, her voice sounding distant, her finger tracing the ring that made up the center of the flower. "It occurs to me, I have no idea who the source really is. Do you?" she caught his green eyes.

"I have a few names that I've heard over the years, but nothin' concrete. Tha's part o' what made Th' Organization work. Secrecy, with only th' most vital connections knowin' all th' details." He indicated the page, "Please, tell us about this."

Smiling shyly, she proceeded to give them her explanation of how all of the parts were aligned.

Finishing a few minutes later, she exhaled loudly. "I have no idea how many of these 'protector' groups are out there. I had heard of the Spiders when I rode with the Dragons, but had never seen them. I guess in a way, I had hoped they weren't real. I guess we'll be lucky if there aren't any more."

"Not that I'm aware of," Brett supplied readily. "But that don't mean that there's not. If there wasn't any need for me t' know about 'em, then I woulda been kept in th' dark; that's th' way o' Th' Organization."

"Right. So they are high on our list of targets. But we need to be clear of the next step before we do anything about them, even if we could locate them at the present. What names did you come up with, as far as the leadership? Who's in charge?" she peered at Brett, then shifted to Mason, hoping one of them had a clue.

"My best guess," the federal agent supplied, "Would be these two guys." Laying another piece of paper on the table, she could see the picture of two very young men.

"Wow, those guys aren't near old enough, I don't think," she conceded.

"Oh, they're old enough. Those pictures are more than 30 years old. And we've been searching… haven't been able to locate any newer ones of them, anywhere, since," he indicated Geek and his handy devices as he spoke.

"Are you sure they're still alive? Maybe they're dead. Maybe that's why there's nothing of them," she played the devil's advocate.

"No, there are a few other records that indicate they're still breathing. They're very particular about hiding, that's all. They're siblings, sons of an old school drug lord who was shot down about the time that those two pictures were taken," he tapped the faces for emphasis.

"Oh wow, they learned from a master, then perfected the whole operation," she breathed.

"We think the same thing. This," he touched the older of the two, "Is Pablo Contreras, and this is his younger brother, Saul Martin Contreras."

She lifted the page, staring at their dark eyes. "I have an idea." She twirled around, reaching for their package and pulling out the files, "We made a copy of Godfry's Rolodex."

"You really thinks they're gonna be in there?" Enrique scoffed.

"No, I think they are *not* going to be in there. Here," she handed out the other files that were clipped in groups according to their original folders, "Flip through and see what names you find. See if you find these two, or anyone else that looks interesting." Turning the pages to the cards, she found nothing close to either of the two men. "Not here, that's a good sign."

"I don't understand why that's a good sign. You're not making any sense, and we've been working on this for hours," Mason's voice was strained, his fatigue glaringly obvious.

"I realize that, but we have to move fast. They're going to shut you two out of the system at any moment, so we have to get what we can before that happens. Did anyone else find anything?" she addressed the group of searchers, accepting the pages from them.

"Look, Tori; the key here is, we need to stay focused. I agree that these two are important, but I think it's too early to go digging through everything we have, trying to make it fit them," Mason blurted out.

Tori was flipping through what she had been presented, only half listening to him, repeating his words in an offhand manner, "The key here is," *the key here is*... Her mind froze, her eyes shooting up to stare at him, "The key," she breathed barely above a whisper. *Son of a bitch, I forgot about the key.*

"What key?" he demanded, unable to control his displeasure any longer, "I told you, you're not making any sense!"

"Hey," Michael cut in, "It's after midnight, and I think we're all getting tired, and a little bit cranky here. Let's turn in and get some sleep, start fresh in the morning."

Tori lay the pages on the table, her exhaustion catching up to her the instant she thought about going to bed, "Actually, I think that's a very good idea. Maybe I'll make more sense in the morning." She smiled up at the tallest man in their group, reaching over to squeeze his arm, "Thank you for pulling out all of this information, and don't worry. We'll go through all of it, not just picking out the parts that support my theories."

Turning to make her way down the hall, she called over her shoulder, "I guess everyone knows where they're going to crash?" a yawn trailing at the end.

"Yes, ma'am," Michael replied playfully. "We've got it all lined out," closing the door behind them.

Risky Business

"We've got a problem," Eli blurted out, bursting through the door of the cabin the following morning.

Tori turned, holding out her cup to avoid spilling her coffee while taking in his disheveled appearance. "Did you sleep in your car?" she demanded.

"Yes," he supplied, "I always do. And I just got off the phone with Godfry. We touched something or left something out of place, so he knew someone had been there."

Holding up her hand, she cut him off. "Relax, Eli. We knew going to his office was risky business. Take a deep breath, and then you can tell me the rest," she finished, lifting her mug to her lips.

"Alright," he exhaled loudly, "After he had realized someone had been in his office, he went down to security, had them pull up the video surveillance of the entrance. He knows I was there and that I took you with me. It's a good thing you hid the copies, or he would know we have those as well. Long story short, Mason and I are out. We will be arrested on sight, for obstruction of justice."

Tori leaned on the counter, considering the situation. "Give me your phone."

"Why?" he scowled, "What good does that do?" he questioned, presenting the device.

Opening it, she dialed the number of his last incoming call, noting the time, and that he had, in fact, come straight in afterwards. Listening for the ring, she waited, then asked the crisp voice that answered the line, "Can I speak to Jim Godfry, please? Yes, I can hold."

The group of men around her stood waiting to see what she was up to. A moment later, he was on the other end, "Hi, Jim; this is Tori." Her warm greeting was met with silence, "Yes, I'm sure you're pretty stunned to hear from me. I have a proposition for you, and we need to meet in private to discuss it."

"A proposition," he stammered. "Now? After all this time, you're ready to do the right thing?"

She could hear the anger in his voice but didn't bite. "I'm ready to do what I have to do, Jim. Like always. When and where can we meet?" Picking up a pencil, she jotted down the address and time. "See, that wasn't so hard. I'll see you then."

"What the hell did you do that for?" Mason demanded.

"I thought you were going to be less cranky," Tori implored. "You know, after a good night's sleep."

"And I thought you were going to make more sense," he countered evenly.

"I am making sense. Finish your breakfast. We have a lot of work to do this morning before I can meet with Godfry after lunch." She kept her tone even as she placed her empty cup in the sink, heading to the bathroom for a private shower, and in case she needed to vomit.

Returning to the kitchen close to an hour later, she had taken the time to cover her scar with her makeup. Michael watched her, having heard her spasms as, unfortunately, everyone else had as well. "You still look tired, baby girl," he commented in a low voice.

"I know," she confessed. "I need more sleep, but getting down to business is more important." Moving over to the map, she began to break down the necessities, "We need to go through the files we got from Godfry's private stash. We take those, and we compare them to the official documents, looking for discrepancies."

"I'll buy that," Brett agreed. "Whatever's different is probably important."

"I'd like to show you what I gave him as well, if you don't mind," Eli looked nervous. "I wanted to tell you last night, but you said to wait until everyone could hear."

"Alright, show us then," Tori turned her gaze to him.

Lifting the packets, he located the one he needed. "I was told to gather information about some disappearances; young women who have disappeared from a four-hundred square mile geographic location, over a period of about twenty-five years."

"These are some pictures of the young women, all between the ages of fifteen and nineteen."

Michael reached over, fanning the pages, his fingers moving quickly at first, then more slowly. Watching him pull out one in particular, Eli continued, "You see the resemblance?"

"Yes, actually I do. What the hell does this have to do with anything, though?" the crystal blue eyes staring at him from the sheet put him on edge. Looking up at his wife, he asked quietly, "Have you seen these?"

Taking what he offered, she shrugged, "I glanced through them, but I wasn't sure what it was about. I thought maybe it was from when they were trying to identify me."

"We never tried to identify you," Eli stated flatly.

Tori could feel the air hang in her lungs, "I suspected you didn't. That's why you hid my age, so that you could own me. So what does this group of girls mean, then?"

"They're victims," he supplied in a low voice. "All taken, none ever found. Ever. And they all look alike," he hesitated slightly, "They all look like you."

"What do you means, 'looks like' her," Enrique demanded, snatching up one of the photos, and then another. Pouring through the stack, a horrified expression crossed his face, "Fuck me, baby girl, they do alls look like you."

"Ok, Eli," she touched a few of the sheets. "You have my attention. What does it mean? Why did Godfry care about this?"

"I don't know why, he didn't tell me that. Maybe you can ask him when you see him. What I do know, is that I think it's important. Very important. There are almost fifty of them; fifty girls in twenty-five years. And no one has ever been arrested, and no connections made. No real investigation into their disappearances collectively that I could find, either; until Godfry asked me to look into them; discretely."

"Wow," the girl breathed. "That's hot. Ok, we set this on the back burner, and move on, and if it's really significant, I'm sure we'll find some other pieces to the puzzle that connect to it."

Brett nodded, sliding his hand over the copies, "We could, but I don' think we'll have t' wait long. I'm sure this's something t' do with how an' why Eddie Farrell chose you."

"How do you figure?" the girl frowned.

"Well," he lay the page he was holding back on the stack, "If you recall, I tol' you he spent almost a year lookin' for the right girl. I always assumed he chose you for your intellect an' your abilities. This makes me think different; he may've also been searching for certain physical characteristics."

"Oh my God, that actually makes sense!" her voice grew louder. "I bet that's why he was so pissed off that I didn't go into puberty like a normal girl, either."

Eli's brow furrowed, "Why is that?'

"Because, you said all of the girls taken were between 15

and 19 years of age. I still had two years of training to complete *after* I matured," she grinned slightly. "By the time I was ready, I was too old to be one of these girls."

"Why is that important?" Mason cut in, intrigued by her train of thought.

"I have no idea," she sounded breathless, "But it's too many connections not to line up somehow. If the girls were being taken, where were they being taken to? And why? I think if we can discover those answers, we will be a lot closer to finding out what Eddie intended to do with me once I was trained."

"You're talkin' about your purpose as his 'secret weapon' aren't you," Enrique burst into laughter. "I remember that shit. Eddie, talkin' like he was a big shot. Gonna take down The Organization and own it all."

"He did say that. I bet Th' Organization is th' one takin' the girls. He picked you, 'cause you fit th' kind o' girls they would be likely t' take," Brett snapped his fingers as he spoke, "An' you'd be inside."

"And getting inside the flower is the key," she spoke more quietly. "The center of the flower is so well guarded, no one gets in without being invited… or brought in."

The room fell under an eerie silence as the group retraced the morning's discoveries. Glancing around at them, she was ready to ask for a break, "Hey, guys; let's go find a diner and have some lunch. Clear our heads for a bit. When we get back we can plot the disappearances of the girls, and see if that helps us triangulate a position."

"A position for what?" Geek spoke up for the first time in a while, in awe at how much they had learned without a single piece of technology.

"Well, if they're abducting girls, and they're staying within a four-hundred mile radius, I'm sure it's because they're staying close to home. I bet their actual headquarters is inside that area, or not far from it," she sucked on her bottom lip, "I think it's worth looking at, either way."

Michael grinned at his wife with pride, "I think you're right, love. And yes, if you feel like eating, we should go have lunch." Reaching to grasp her hand, he guided her out to his bike, where she took her place behind him.

A Last Goodbye

After lunch, the group returned to the cabin, and Tori rode her bike, only taking Enrique and Michael with her to meet Godfry. Once they were at the location, they pulled up in a row, shutting off their bikes. Surveying their surroundings, she finally sat up straighter on the seat, kicking the bike over easily and listening to it purr for a moment. "Stay here," she commanded. The men glanced at one another, but made no move to disobey.

Easing her ride around the curves, she pulled up behind Godfry's Lincoln Town car and killed the engine. Swinging her leg over, she made her way across the brown grass, unclasping her gloves and shoving them into a pocket. Jim didn't flinch when she cleared her throat, standing beside him.

"I knew you'd come around," he said in a monotone voice. The earth around Debra's gravestone was freshly dug as if it had only recently been set. "I sometimes wonder why she did it."

"Why she did what?" Tori used a soft tone to preserve his mood.

"Why she helped you. She was so… proud… of what she and Eli did for you. I was so angry. They had disobeyed orders. My orders." He heaved a heavy sigh; his round belly lifting and falling in the process. "I punished them for it. Both of them. I sent Eli off to handle Dominguez. I put

80

Debra on suspension. She never forgave me. Things were never the same between us after that."

Tori shifted, uncomfortable with the tear that rolled down his pudgy cheek. "You told them not to help me?"

"No. They were allowed to help you. They weren't supposed to get too close to you. It was supposed to be… business." He shrugged; the recollection clouded by time. "Eli should have been a professional. I'm sorry that he wasn't."

"I'm not upset about what happened between us," Tori countered, "I needed him. It helped me that he cared about me when he did. I'm not sure I would have ever made it out of that hospital if he hadn't."

"Oh, you would've made it out," Jim chuckled. "You're a strong woman. Had to be to have survived all those years." He shifted, turning his gaze to look at her, wiping the streaks from his face. "I tried to be strong, like you. Did everything I could to control things. To make things be the way I wanted them to be."

Holding an open palm towards the mound of dirt, "This is what it got me. And after she died, my wife discovered our affair and our marriage ended in divorce," his laughter sounded hollow. "So I lost two women over one little mistake."

"Whose mistake," Tori prodded. "What happened?"

"Mine," he stated sharply. "Although there were plenty of others who made mistakes as well. Mine was the one that mattered. You see, I let them push me. Only once, but once was enough. And after you cross that line…," he chuckled again, "There's no putting it back. You can draw another line, and you can say to yourself, '*this time, I'm not going to budge.*' But that new line isn't as strong as the first one, and it falls even quicker."

Tori inhaled deeply, fear wrenching her gut, "Are you

working for The Organization?" She instantly regretted the question, but it was too late to withdraw it.

The pause was long, before he nodded his head, looking off in the distance. "Some would say so. It really depends on which line you want to talk about. All I ever really did was look the other way. Closed the file. That's all it took, and everything I have worked my whole life for slipped away."

"What file, Jim?" she barely whispered.

"Castleford. That's the name the original case fell under. The day after Bradley Wells was found, I got a phone call. A complete stranger, who made me an offer. It's not like I hadn't been contacted before. But that time was different." He was shaking his head at the memory, as if to change it somehow. "I didn't take the bribe," he cut his eyes over at her, "But I might as well have."

"What did you do if you didn't take it?" her lip quivered slightly, his pain evident and pouring over her.

He shrugged, "I took a few days, made like we were searching for new leads. Let everyone think we were continuing the fight," he rocked his head in an exaggerated manner. "But I was tired. Tired of the game, tired of the dead ends and brick walls. Losing another agent was more than I could bear. So, I closed the file. I let it go," he raised his hands, opening a palm as if he were pitching the folder to the wind all over again. "Then you turned up, not dead in a house full of dead men."

"And I got an idea. See, after I helped them, the phone calls kept coming. Things they wanted and I was supposed to provide. Like I closed the case *for them*," his voice picked up an angry tone, his hands clenched into fists. "They pushed me, making demands. At first I tried to fight it, but what was the use?"

"Jesus," Tori swore under her breath.

"No, even he couldn't help me at that point. I was sunk.

When you came into the picture, that was the only hope I had," he looked over at her, doleful blue eyes blinking slowly, "You killed the Dragons. All by yourself. Eddie Farrell raised you, taught you everything you know. The more we learned about you, the more sure I was that *you* could put an end to my problems."

Tori gritted her teeth, biting back the words she wanted to fling at him.

Seeing her jaw flex, he smiled, "That's why I kept suggesting you go after them. I needed you to save me."

"I'm not here to save you," she spoke bitterly. "And Debra's death and Doug's death, and everyone in between; their blood is on your hands."

"I know," he didn't bother to argue. "I've reached the end of what I can do. For all my pushing, all my conniving, it hasn't gotten me anywhere." He paused, squinting at her, as if she were out of focus, "What is it that you want? I know you're not here because you give a rat's ass about me."

Tori shifted, uncomfortable with his confessions. Wrinkling her nose at him, she asked in a submissive voice, "Did you tell The Organization about me? Did you sell me out?"

"Sell you out?" he choked on the words. "What good would that have done? I wanted you to finish them. You couldn't do that if I told them about you." He slid his tongue over his teeth, "No one was more disappointed about Doug than I was, and for that very reason. They didn't know anything about you really until they got to him."

Her face crinkled; she pursed her lips, "I need my clothes. My jacket to be precise."

"Your jacket? You're wearing your jacket," he muttered.

"Not this one. The one I wore when I rode with the Dragons. The one that was in the house when we were found. Eli says it could be in evidence somewhere. But, since you have ostracized both him and Mason, I have to ask you for it." She stared at him, waiting for his response. "They are good men, Jim. You shouldn't punish them for helping do this thing that you want done so badly."

"I won't," he shook his head. "I had to shut them out, but their records will be cleared if you are successful. I'll see to that. As far as your clothes," he shrugged, "I know where they might be. We gathered everything from the house and had it boxed. It's all in the evidence vault at the warehouse. You'll have to go through it to find what you need."

"And how will we get into the vault?"

"I'll get you a window. No one can know that you were there. Take Eli, he'll know where to go and where to look. Tell him I'll clear the path. You won't have long, thirty minutes at most, so be quick." He gave her a small grin, "I'm glad you finally decided to take care of them. Whatever your reasons, I hope you make it."

"Yeah, that makes two of us," she half grinned herself. "What time?"

"Nine, in the morning," he nodded, "You'll be fine. And good luck to you on all that comes after that." Turning, he walked away, leaving the girl standing at the grave of her friend.

Tori let him go, her mind drifting over the memories of Debra; what she had meant to her. "Goodbye, my friend," she called softly to the marble, "I swear they will go down, or we will. I can't let this go any longer." Turning, she made her way back to her bike, starting it and setting off to rejoin the rest of her crew and give them her news.

Gather the Evidence

The following morning, Eli drove her to the warehouse that Godfry had spoken of. To his surprise, the attendant at the gate swung it open for them without argument. His expression placid, he parked in front of the plain brown structure and led her inside. Within minutes, they were on the proper floor and had located the section of items taken from the farmhouse, over twenty boxes in all.

"Wow, I'm sure it'll be here," he speculated. "It looks like they collected anything that appeared to belong to the Dragons."

"I think you're right," she hoisted a box and sat it on the floor, tossing the lid off and rummaging inside. "It's a black leather jacket, with silver buttons. Looks a lot like the one I'm wearing, too." Nodding, he set about helping her.

The process continued for several minutes, each of them taking down totes to gaze inside. Finally, Eli flipped open a lid and could feel his pulse quicken. Lifting the black leather, he called to her, "Hey, I think this might be it."

Tori shoved a plastic bag she had been inspecting into her pocket. Joining him, she held up the heavy material, recalling the day it was presented to her. "Yeah, this was mine," she breathed as she lay it over the box, her hands squeezing it, feeling for the object she had hidden inside the lining.

"We need any of this other stuff?" he glanced around

them at the other boxes, with their contents pulled out and scattered.

"No, you can put it all back," she had located the small piece of metal and was preparing to cut it out with a blade from her boot. "This is what we came for," she held up the shiny silver key for him to see before she placed it in her pocket, shoving the mutilated outerwear back into storage.

"So what does it go to?" he inquired, quickly cleaning their mess.

"I have no idea," she confessed.

Eli stopped moving to glare at her, "You mean we came to get a key, and you have no idea what it opens?"

"Yup," she tossed back, placing the last box on the shelf. "That's it, let's get the hell out of here."

Leaving the room, the pair stepped onto the elevator, the doors closing as he hit the button that would take them to the ground floor. "You're only saying you don't know because you don't trust me."

Cutting her eyes over at him, she heaved a deep breath, forcing the air out noisily, "I trust you. I really don't know. I do know that whatever it fits is important. I'm certain this is what Eddie was searching for the night he killed Henry. I thought it might go to the toolbox from his storage; the one that held his cash stores."

She paused as they exited the cubicle and made their way out the front doors unchecked. Her heels clicking loudly on the sidewalk, they climbed into his car, and she continued, "But it couldn't be the box. Eddie had his own cash, and that wouldn't be important enough to kill a member of the crew. Plus, Henry concealed the fact that he gave it to me, which is why I hid it myself, and didn't tell anyone that I had it."

"Well," Eli replied, his nerves calming as the building faded behind them, "When we meet up with the others, we can brainstorm some ideas of what it might unlock."

Tori watched the familiar buildings zooming past, "Yeah, and until we do, I'll keep it safe." Patting her pocket, she remembered the evidence bag she had also removed from one of the boxes. Pulling it out, her fingers slid over the smooth surface.

She lifted the plastic, staring at the knife through the hazy covering. Unzipping the seal, she slid the shiny metal out onto her hand, rubbing the cold steel as the memories cascaded around her.

TORI… the engraving was still visible. *Eddie's gift to me.* She thought about the day he gave her the blade. *The day after he raped me, and marked me.* Her hand moved uncontrollably up to caress the bite mark she had covered with Michael's name.

Her mind became trapped in the past, and she considered the gift itself. *He must have bought it sometime before that… would have had to.* Prepared it and kept it, waiting to present it to her as Michael had done with his ring. *How long had he waited? What was he waiting for?*

Tori recalled that Eddie had not allowed any man to touch her. *Not until I was ready. Matured.* Or was it something else he waited for? *"Eddie wants to be your first, baby girl."* That's what Henry had told her.

Shifting in the seat, she recalled the training and the time that she had spent with the leader of their group. Never patient, always demanding. Demanding what? *Touching me, stroking my hair. Always innocent, never a hand where it shouldn't have been.* So why did it bother her so much? He was such an evil man, *what was he waiting for?* Why didn't he take her then, and get it over with?

Turning the knife in her hand, the truth began to flicker in the back of her mind. *He was waiting for you. For you to choose.* Eddie wanted the girl for his own. The knife was a special gift, marked with her name. *He wanted me to be his mate.* Did Eddie Farrell love her? Is that why they had played their game?

But, he was terrible to me. Always! She recalled the beatings she had taken from him, dimly aware that no one else had been permitted to raise a hand to her back in the day. It wasn't until after her induction that Red had been permitted to unleash his dark and morbid desires upon her.

And Eddie played the good guy. Coming along behind his brother, holding me tenderly, soothing my wounds. Trying to make things better, but things were never better. *I hated him the same; never wanted to be with him.*

The light snapped on brightly; *he was waiting for you to choose him!* But she didn't choose Eddie… she chose Henry. *Henry was my first.*

"What's that?" Eli interrupted her thoughts, causing her to jump.

"It's nothing," she breathed, "My old knife. The one that Eddie gave me when I was inducted."

She ran her thumb across her name again, *I never understood before.* She felt a stab of sadness that she had missed out on this detail and the significance of it. *Would it have changed anything, if I had known? Would it have mattered, if I had chosen him?*

Says Who

Arriving back at the camp, Tori made her way into the cabin and closed the door to the bedroom, stretching out across the bed. Reaching into her inner pocket, she pulled out the knife, turning the talisman in her hand as if it were capable of transporting her into the past. Breathing deeply, she focused on Eddie, rifling through the memories.

After they had inducted her, the rest of the group partook of her at will. However, she was rarely made to service them all in the same night, unless she needed to be punished. Outsiders to the group were only permitted to touch with permission; Eddie's permission.

Of course, there were only perhaps a dozen men outside the Dragons and the Scorpions that she had ever been with. Eddie liked his prize and only shared her if the recipient was highly deserving. Her mind going over those who had made the cut, she came across Bradley Wells. He was not so worthy, and the reason she had been shared with him was dark.

Tori had been outside, with the rest of the Dragons, when they received their orders regarding him, so she had no idea what was actually said. All she knew was what Eddie had told her; that he was a Fed, which turned out to have been true. At the time, she hadn't really cared about the secret meetings where the leader and his second would disappear into the shop to meet with the rep.

Her mind skipping forward; she smiled slightly, recalling that she had accompanied Brett to such a meeting, during the time that she was his second. She had half expected the rep to turn her away; women held no rank among the groups that work for The Organization.

Bolting straight up, Tori's mind froze, *oh my God!* Digging in her pocket, she fumbled for the key, pulling it out and staring at it. Turning it slowly in her fingers, she recalled the room, standing next to Brett and wearing her somber disguise. Along one of the walls there stood a filing cabinet. She recalled wondering at the time what could be inside it.

Staring at the object, she continued to scour the memory, *you can't pick the lock on a file cabinet. They're too hard; virtually impossible.* Smiling to herself, *you have to have the key, or a drill, to get inside.* Leaping off the bed, she bolted into the front room, "I know what the key fits!"

The men of her crew were scattered about the room, shocked at her unexpected interruption. "What key?" Michael demanded calmly.

"This key," she held it up so that they could see. "This's what was in my jacket; the item Eli and I had to retrieve," She grinned eagerly, ready to share. "I didn't want you to think I was silly, going to get it..." she paused, seeing the smirk on the agent's face, "You already told them."

"Well, you didn't say not to," he defended. "And we were talking about what it might go to, but it would appear that you figured it out." He crossed his hands into his lap, "So what does it fit?"

"A file cabinet," she was a bit breathless at the revelation.

"A file cabinet?!?" Brett's voice was loud. "Why th' hell would that be -" he stopped speaking in mid-sentence, his jaw dropped slightly, "In th' meeting rooms, with th' reps," he finished.

"Exactly," she smiled at him. "The one in Miami has one. I remember seeing it when we were there."

Standing, he shook his head, reaching to grasp the shiny object. "They all have 'em," his voice was low, considering all the rooms he had been in. "No one but group leaders an' their seconds are allowed in th' rooms, neither." Holding the key up to the light, as if he could see through it, he grunted, "So which city does this key fit?"

"I don't think it fits any of them. I think it goes to a box at their headquarters, where ever that is," her eyes twinkled.

"Ok, first offs, anything important don't gos in a filing cabinet," Enrique input, less than diplomatically. "Important stuff goes in a safe."

Brett released a low whistle, "There's no safe in th' meeting rooms. At leas', not visible. An' safes are heavy. File cabinets, you can move. Or bolt 'em t' th' wall, if ya wants." He blew air out through his pursed lips, running his fingers through his red curls. "I'm at a loss here."

Michael moved in beside him to take the key. Turning it to peer at both sides, he postulated, "So Eddie got ahold of this, somehow, but Henry ended up with it. This little... thing... is the reason my brother is dead."

Tori's smile slowly faded, gripped by the thought that he was exactly right. Furthermore, if she had spoken up the night of their fight, and handed it over, he might not have been killed. Closing her eyes, she shuddered, recalling the way Red had held her, preventing her from trying to intervene.

His eyes shifting to meet hers, his mood was hard to read. "Here," he held it out to her, "Keep it safe. If it meant enough to him to die for, it must be pretty important, whatever it opens and whatever is inside alike."

"Man this is getting us no wheres," Enrique continued his negativity.

Turning to look at him, the lines sank into Michael's forehead, "What the hell, Enrique? You have a better plan? You have information to share? Otherwise, shut the fuck up."

Tori stared at her mate, her mouth gaping open. "I've never heard you speak to anyone like that, Michael Anderson!"

Not taking his eyes off the other man, he clenched his jaw, "Well, I warned you, I'm not really the nice guy you think I am." Turning his back on the group, he made his way out onto the porch, slamming the door behind him.

Tori reached over, slapping Enrique on the arm, "What the hell is the matter with you? Can't you see he's upset? Eddie murdered his brother over that key, and we're making the progress we can make. Quit being a prick!" Reaching the door, she closed it behind her, only a bit more gently than her mate. Standing beside him, she gazed out into the afternoon sun.

"Sorry," he apologized immediately, "I know that was uncalled for."

"Don't worry about it, love," she shook her dark waves. "I know things are tough all around."

"Yeah," he agreed, shoving his hands into his pockets, "But it's more than we had. I think we need to move though, within a day, two at the most. I figure we're only staying ahead of The Organization by a narrow margin at best. I don't like being this close to Godfry either, since they have their hooks in him."

"Absolutely," she whispered, sliding her hand up his back. "I'm going back inside. Join us when you feel like it." She gave him a small smile; his creamy orbs drawing her in for a moment and causing her to long for home. Leaning forward, she tasted his lips, her nose grazing his cheek before she stepped away, closing the door much more gently this time behind her.

Eddie's Girl

Rejoining the rest of her crew, Tori called them to order, "I'd like to have a brief meeting. We need to discuss our next move."

"Yes, ma'am," Enrique mocked her with a salute, still angry at their altercation.

Giving him a shake of her head, she ignored his unhappiness, "I was thinking about the Dragons. That's how I determined what the key is for. I believe that Eddie knew where their headquarters were located, as well as some of the particulars of how they functioned." She frowned slightly, "I also think we're on the right track as far as the girls are concerned."

"What we need to do is to determine how we're going to locate the Spiders so we can eliminate them. We also need to plot the locations of the abductions on the map here, zero in on the center of The Organization. And finally, we need to devise a way to either solidify or eliminate the Contreras brothers as the head of the group." She looked up as Michael joined them, giving him a small smile.

"I don't think it matters who's in charge," he jumped into the conversation. "If we can locate them, we'll take them out, no matter who they are."

"True," she nodded her agreement, "But knowing may give us further insight into formulating our plans. And since Godfry seems to think working in teams and delegating tasks helps, I'd like to give that a try."

Lifting the bundles of pages, she held one of them out to Eli, "You've already spent a great deal of time on this material. What I'd like is for you and Michael to plot these on the map to see what that gets us." Eli accepted the pages, giving the taller man a silent glare.

"You two," she indicated Enrique and Brett, "Are on Spider detail. You know the most out of everyone here about who they are and how working for The Organization looks and feels. Come up with everything you can that will help us find that crew."

"And finally," she handed the remaining stack of papers to Geek, "I need you and Mason to go through these. I don't care which, either make it definite or eliminate them, but I'm sure there's evidence as to who's in charge in all this... stuff. And, you have the Rolodex copies. You can pull up all of those numbers, see if you can find out who all of those people are and where to find them."

"If we can get all of this together by tonight, we'll be in great shape. I want to be able to leave here in the morning, regardless, and this will give us some indication of which way we should go," she took a seat on a stool as she finished.

"I notice you're not on a team," Eli pointed out.

"No, this way I can move between you guys and help out where ever I'm needed," she supplied smoothly.

"Or, you can go get some rest," Brett reached out, clasping her arm and practically shoving her off her seat towards the bedroom.

"What the hell?" she stammered. "Who says I need a nap?"

"I do," he insisted. "Your ol' man is bein' nice about it. I have less need t' be subtle; you look like shit. You're exhausted, an' you need t' take care o' yourself. Don' worry about all o' this," he waved his hand around at the clutter;

"We got our assignments an' we'll take care of 'em. We'll wake you this evenin'. Now go!" he waved her towards the back.

Standing, the girl thought she might argue, but her drooped frame was attracted to the idea of climbing into bed as if it were a magnet. "Alright," she peered around to see they were all indicating their agreement via nods and grins. "I'll go then. But please come and get me if you need anything."

"No worries, baby girl. We will," her mate took her by the hand and guided her across the floor, kissing her at the doorway before closing it.

Alone in the back room, she kicked off her boots and stretched out on top of the blankets, thinking it was silly and would probably take an hour for her head to stop spinning enough to sleep. *There's so much to do, and so many things I hadn't put together before.* In the end, her fatigue won, and she passed out almost as soon as her head hit the pillow.

Darkness had already engulfed the tiny room when she awoke with a start, clearly several hours later. Her pulse in her throat, she could recall the terror of her nightmare and was reminded of the one she had had before in New Jersey. *When Michael was gone; or hurt.* Only this time, it wasn't her mate she had been searching for.

Rising, she flicked on the light to chase away the shadows, and made her way to the bathroom that stood in the hallway, grateful that it lay between the front and back halves of the cabin, doors on each side that made it private from either direction. Washing her face with cold water, her pulse began to slow.

She hated the fact that she had dreamed of Enrique, something she had done a few times since his return. *This time was worse, though;* she rationalized. This time, she had been afraid of losing him, *maybe because he was angry with me.* Opening the door that led out to the others, she wiped the emotion from her face, "You guys let me sleep too long."

"Naw," Brett countered with a grin, "We got a lot done, an' you needed th' rest."

"Do I still look like shit?" she demanded bluntly.

"Not so much," he chuckled. "We made dinner and kept a plate for ya. And we're ready t' brief you on what we've come up with." Clearing a spot for her at the table, the teams prepared to make their presentations.

She took her seat, and Michael placed her meal before her, running his fingers through her hair, "Eat what you can, love. You need your strength." His smile looked strained, and for a moment it appeared as if he were going to say more, before he forced a larger grin and backed away.

"Ok," he called loudly, "I think Eli and I will go first. We plotted the locations on the map, and he was right, they all fall within a certain geographic location, but we noticed something else, too. Eleven of them took place in a single spot, over the period of years."

Tori gasped, "They all lived in the same place?"

"No, they didn't live in the same place, they were all in the same bar. Taken from it." Arm extended, he lay his finger on the map, where a thick cluster of red dots had been made, surrounded by others on the map. "Each dot represents an abduction. This group of girls was taken from here, one a yearish, at almost the same time. Which makes me think that perhaps the years that one wasn't taken, one actually was, but we don't know about them."

Tori could feel the hairs on the back of her neck standing on end, "Girls who look like me."

"Yes, very much like you," Eli spoke up. "I think you are exactly right, and that's how Eddie intended to get you inside. All he had to do was have you at the bar, at the right time, and it's all but a given you would have been taken.

Why he backed out, it's hard to say. Except that you're right, you were too old by the time you were ready. That and you're too tall."

"Too tall? What does that have to do with it?"

"You're a good six inches taller than the next closest of the abductees. Eddie probably had no way of knowing how big you were going to get when he chose you," her husband supplied. "I'm sure that was part of his frustration. You told me that he came back every year, upset that you hadn't matured. I think he was more unhappy that you were still growing."

"I see," she curled her tongue as she considered the theory. "It's all good then. We may still be able to use the location if we need to. If they don't take me, they will take another girl, and that could lead us to their headquarters either way. Timing could be a factor, but at least it's an option"

"Agreed," the two men said almost simultaneously, casting a frown at one another afterwards.

"I guess we could go next," Geek spoke up. "Not that we have much to report, as far as the Rolodex goes. All of the numbers checked out. They're all agents, and they're based out of different branches. Mason was able to verify some of them, and there didn't appear to be any irregularities in that regard. If Godfry has been contacting The Organization, he didn't leave their number around where we could find it."

"And that takes us to the second part of our task," Mason took over, "The Contreras brothers *are* our most likely suspects. Their father was killed by a rival group of drug lords, or so we thought, as that's what the history in the file would indicate. However, at the same time that it happened, these two disappeared," he indicated the pair by laying their pictures on top of the map. "Making his murder look more like an inside job."

"At the same time, another pair of men appeared, and we do have a few pictures of them. This," he lay a picture next to one of the brothers, "Is Rico Ramirez. See the similarities? We put it through the facial recognition database, and the system kicked it back... ninety-eight percent chance that it's the same guy. And this," he lay down the second photograph, "This is Ruben Ramirez. He was ninety-nine percent, and we ran the search blind. The computer pulled up the matches without us having to indicate what we suspected."

"Wow," Tori breathed, "I don't think you can argue with that."

"No, you can't," Mason agreed. "Unfortunately, they have kept themselves out of the spotlight since they changed their identities, and seem to be pretty normal guys. You ready for this? They own houses in El Paso and Juarez, and have nothing on their records whatsoever."

Tori's eyes flicked over to the map. "El Paso? The bar is in El Paso, the one that all the girls disappear from."

"I wondered if you would notice that," he grinned broadly, holding up an index finger. "So I have one last thing to share. Before their father was murdered, he took care of some charges for one of his sons. It seems that Pablo, aka Rico, was arrested... for abducting, raping, and beating a girl to death. Black hair, blue eyes, sixteen years old." Tori's gaze shot up to meet his, her chest heaving. "Kind of takes your breath away, doesn't it?" he finished with a nod.

"No shit," she gasped. "This's amazing. We've got these guys!"

"Not yet, we haven't," Brett cut her off, "But we're close." Stepping up to the table, he swung his hand over the map. "You know as well as th' rest of us that th' Spiders, like all o' th' groups that they control, move as a pack. Here and there," he tapped a few places on the map, "They meet with reps, who give them orders an' they take care o' business."

"Yes, I know that," Tori sighed, "What's your point?"

"So, we wanna set a trap for 'em," he appeared elated.

"Set a trap for them? And how exactly are we going to do that?" she demanded.

"We marked all four o' th' rep locations on th' map. I'm sure you're familiar with them already; Miami, Denver, LA, an' New York. What we wanna do is attack one of 'em. Wipe 'em out. Plus, we can crack open that file cabinet, t' check it out, in case it does contain anything o' value," he paused, allowing her to mull over his plan.

"Then we smashs whoever shows up," Enrique growled with a rumble of laughter.

"You think it'll be the Spiders?" she reached out, touching the green dot in New York.

"Doesn't matter, we're gonna kills whoever it is. And if it's not them, we'll either waits there for them, or heads towards the next dot; you know they'll shows up eventually," Enrique's brown eyes shone.

"No," she tapped the map, "I say we hit them all. Every location."

"How the hells are we going to do that? There's only sevens of us, counting the computer nerd," he flicked his chin at Geek. "And they're spread all across the country. I mean, there's only fours, but there's no way we could make it to all of them. It would take days, and they would be ready for us."

"Not if we use the plane," she supplied in a quiet voice. "We have a private jet, and a locker full of supplies in each of these cities."

The room fell silent, the group stunned by the boldness of her plan. Finally, Michael spoke up, "How long would it take to carry that out? And what about our bikes? We make a loop, ending up back where we started?"

Tori nodded; her eyes fixed on the map and mentally

making the trip. "We land and purchase or rent vehicles in each of the towns. We have huge cash stores at each of the locations, so we could do either. And Brett has the list of the munitions we will find in each as well. We load up what we need; we hit them and fly out. Fast. Twenty-four hours, round trip."

She began to nod, the entire plan taking shape. "Denver is our starting point," she pointed her finger over the map, indicating each of the stops. "Over to LA, across to New York, south to Miami, and back to Denver. There, we get on our bikes, and we head south, to El Paso."

"But if we eliminate them, the branches; why wouldn't we waits for the Spiders to come to us?" Enrique wrinkled his nose in confusion.

"Cause, ol' Rico an' Ruben won' send 'em after us," she sneered in a southern drawl. "They're going to be scared shitless. Plus, there won't be any reps to give the orders. If they're able to contact the group, they'll call them in, for added protection, in case we're able to get to them."

"But if we do that, they won't take a girl from the bar..." Eli's voice trailed away, "We don't need them to take anyone. We already know where they are."

"Exactly," she thumped the map, "And we're going to take them apart, one piece at a time. Michael, I need you to be in charge of the plane. You secure the pilots and file the flight plans, one leg at a time, and only at the last possible minute, in case anyone is watching us. The longest leg of the flight is LA to New York, but only about six hours. I think we'll be ok with that."

"Damn right we will be," Mason agreed wholeheartedly. "This sounds very doable. Eddie Farrell taught you well, baby girl."

"Yeah, well, you know," she countered with a grin, "I always was Eddie's girl."

My Side of the Law

Tori felt oddly euphoric entering their room. She had ordered everyone to get some sleep, and was looking forward to the time alone with her mate. They would break camp in the morning, making the day's journey to Denver directly, and they would have less time to themselves. Stripping off her clothes, she pondered if this would be their last chance to lie together as husband and wife.

"You know, this has the potential to get ugly," Michael warned, not moving to join her. Tori turned, standing in her bra and panties to glare at him, feeling deflated by his tone as he went on, "And I don't just mean for them. Some of us could be hurt… or killed. And if we're successful, we more than likely will do time for this."

Tori stopped moving, feeling a surge of anger, unable to control it. "Do time for this?" she scoffed. "I've been flirting with prison my whole life, and I haven't landed there yet. Besides, this is what Godfry wants. I'm sure if we make it, he'll cover it for us, like he already has."

"Maybe," her mate confessed, moving close enough to rake a few fingers across her bare flesh, "But we have so much at stake here."

"You're not going to chicken out on me are you?" she demanded crossly. "What happened to, 'I'm not the nice guy you think I am'? You made it sound like you're a badass, but you're coming across as a wimp," she sputtered.

"I'm not a wimp," he tossed back at her, his voice elevated. "But I do have lots to consider, you for one. I don't want anything to happen to you…" he paused, taking in her tall frame with a low glare, "Or anyone else."

"Well, don't worry about me… or anyone else," she snapped. "This is my side of the law. The ugly dark side, where people get hurt, and end up dead. You wanted to be here, and I'm fine with that, but you can't let your emotions get in the way. You have to be ready to act and do whatever it takes to get the job done. You got it?"

"Yeah, I got it," he exhaled loudly. "You know, you're awfully moody lately. I think those pills of yours are effecting you. Maybe you should quit taking them."

"Quit taking them?" she cried in horror. "Are you crazy? I could get pregnant if I don't. You want that to happen?"

He chuckled, "Not right this minute, no. But I think you need to be a little more level headed. Where're the pills? I want to see them."

Tori stared at him, mouth hanging open wide, "The pills are my business, Michael."

"Wrong," he corrected her firmly, "You're my wife, and that makes them my business, too." Spinning around, he grabbed her bag and began to rummage through it while she reached out, flailing her arms and trying to stop him. Locating the case, he pulled it out and stared at the nearly empty package.

Seeing that there was only one partial row of pills left, twenty-one pink ones, he quickly calculated that she had enough left to take her just beyond her visit with the doctor, if she made it to see him. That and there was one green one. *She missed her period;* he gripped the package tighter. *I knew it.*

Crinkling it, he stuffed it into his pocket. "I'm keeping these. You don't need the rest," he commanded stiffly.

"Give those back!" Tori demanded, slapping him on the arm. "I'm supposed to be taking those!"

"Not anymore," he breathed. "And don't worry about getting pregnant... I'm not going to touch you." His voice was barely above a whisper, feeling as if he might be sick himself.

Her jaw dropped, "Oh, that's *great*, Michael! What the hell are you doing and *why* are you doing it now?!?"

"Because I have to," he held his feelings in check. "Get some sleep, love. I'm going to go outside, so you can rest." He dropped her pack, backing towards the door.

Her brow furrowed, eyes instantly full of tears, "You mean you're not even going to stay in here with me?"

"Do you want me to stay?"

"Yes, I want you to stay! You're my husband, remember? Love of my life, and all that shit," she tossed at him, catching the tear as it streaked down her cheek with a trembling palm.

"Alright, I'll stay," he chuckled, moving forward to catch her in an embrace. "Don't cry, love. Everything's going to be fine. I promise." Clutching his jacket, she buried her face in the leather and breathed deeply, lost in the scent.

"I'm sorry I'm so emotional," she huffed into his neck. "Maybe you're right. Maybe I should stop taking them. They could be the reason I've been sick, too."

"Yeah, maybe they are," he agreed quietly, his fingers tracing the line of her back. "Let's go to bed," he pressed his lips into her hair. "We've got a big couple of days coming up, and we're going to need the sleep." Stepping back, she allowed him to remove his clothes while she covered herself with a cotton tee and slid beneath the covers.

Switching off the light, Michael took his place beside her, pulling her against his bare chest. Catching her fingers as they sifted lightly through the hairs, he sighed against the top of her head. "Good night, baby girl."

"I think we should make love," she countered softly.

"Make love?" he whispered back. "Now?"

"Yes, now," she stated firmly, pushing herself up onto an elbow, "After tonight… we may not get another chance."

He could see the outline of her against the light of the window behind her. Grasping a few hairs, he soothed, "You have to believe we're going to make it through this."

"But what if we don't," her dreams haunted her. "What if this is the last chance we have to hold each other?" Her voice shook slightly, her feelings still raw and oozing out of her. Pushing her over, he sat up, climbing above her and sliding her shirt up and out of the way.

Her nipples were dark against her creamy flesh; a soft glow cast on them by the moonlight. His nose nuzzled her rose briefly before his lips and tongue found the hardened tip, teasing it lightly. His hands caressed her curves as his mouth moistened a trail down to her navel, and across the delicate skin that led to her womanhood below.

His hand on her inner thigh, he guided her legs apart, digits raking across the hairs and folds, slithering their way inside her. His teeth bit at her gently, causing her to breathe sporadically. He had always had a way with her, and this night was no exception, driving her along, her fingers worming their way through his curls and pressing against his scalp. Moments later, she trembled violently, pulling at his sandy locks until she was no longer able.

Snaking his way back up her body, he pulled his briefs aside and plunged himself into her warm wetness. Kissing her jaw, he found her mouth, and she parted her lips so their tongues could mingle while he drove into her in harder strokes. Looping his fingers with hers, he lifted her hands over her head, pinning her playfully, continuing to taste and bite while he moved against her to completion.

His own grip growing lax, he panted into the pillow next to her head, the weight of him pressing down on her completely. "I love you, Tori," he swallowed visibly. "If this was the last time I will ever have you, I want you to know, there will never be another." Her hands released; she pushed them into his curls once more.

"Oh, Michael," she breathed, her voice choked with emotion. Blinking rapidly, her fingers found his face. She caressed the line of his jaw and the stubble that he roughed against her nether regions only moments before. She couldn't bring herself to say more, as much as she wished she could tell him that he was her one and only.

There was a time in her past that she might have, and not given the words a second thought, as she had when she played Eddie to be her fool. But at that moment, she could feel the presence of another man, lurking in the shadows of her heart, and she was riddled with guilt that she could not say that she was his and his alone. Sufficing herself to cling to him, she hoped that he would understand.

Stand or Fold

The following morning, the group awoke early. Putting on his jeans, Michael left his wife to shower and get ready, taking her container of pills and closing the door behind him. In the kitchen area, the rest of the guys were milling around, making coffee and cooking breakfast. Taking out a plastic cup, he filled it half full of water and began dropping the pills into it, one by one.

Turning from his position at the stove, Enrique watched his hands for a moment, before he asked, "Why are you doing that? Are those what I thinks they are?"

"Yeah, they're what you think they are," Michael cut his eyes up at the other man calmly. "And she doesn't need them anymore, so I'm getting rid of them."

"She told you that? That she's..." he hesitated, looking around to see who else was listening.

"No, she doesn't know," he swirled the glass for a few seconds, then dumped it down the sink, running the water behind it.

"Doesn't know what?" Geek joined the conversation, "That she's pregnant? How can she not know?"

"Shhh," Michael held his hand up, "Keep your voice down. She just doesn't. She thinks she's sick, and I want it to stay that way. Finding out will only complicate things; make this whole mess harder for her to get through."

"Wow, that's pretty means, don' ya think?" Enrique

challenged.

"No, it isn't. She needs a clear head right now, and worrying about the future isn't conducive to that." He cast a glance around the group, rocking his jaw side to side. "I do have a favor to ask, though."

Enrique went back to stirring his eggs, "What kinda favor?" He didn't bother to look at the other man. They were only friends for her sake, and it was too early in the day to pretend otherwise.

"I want you to take care of her," Michael waited, nodding his sandy curls when the man's dark eyes swung back to him. "Yeah, if I don't make it through this, I need to know someone is going to look after her."

"Why me?" Enrique demanded, not sure if this was some kind of trick, "Are you offering me your wife?"

Michael pursed his lips, aware that everyone in the room was listening, the silence deafening. Hearing his bride coughing through the thin paneling on the wall, he nodded. "I guess that I am. She has a thing for you. I don't know how deep it goes, but I know that she would let you, you know… take care of her."

He shrugged as he spoke, nervous after he had been so bold, at what it might mean in the end. "I need to know that if I don't make it back that she'll be ok."

"She'll be fine," Eli cut in, "You know, you two aren't the only ones that care about her. She's got a whole room full of men here who would love to look after her."

Enrique and Michael shifted their gaze to the shorter man, breaking into grins and then exchanging a look as if they knew a secret they weren't about to share. "Alright," the dark-haired man agreed, "If anything happens to you, consider it done. And if I don't make it," he snickered, "Then you gets a turn," he waved his spatula at Eli.

"You guys're weird, ya know that?" Brett burst into the

conversation, "We're all gonna make it, and everything's gonna be fine. So get your shit together so we can get th' hell outta here."

Exiting the bathroom and joining them a short time later, Tori had applied the makeup to cover her scar; an effort to lift her spirits by 'feeling' pretty. Almost immediately, a plate heaping with scrambled eggs and bacon was placed in front of her, which she waved at profusely, "Oh, no, please get that outta my face. I'll take a piece of toast."

The laughter and chatter died away at her request; her food was exchanged for browned bread, and the group ate quietly. Noticing the silence, she tried to fill the void, "From here we need to head to Denver. That's the one vault that you guys didn't have access to, because it belonged to Henry. And, I've already cleaned out the funds that were in it."

"There's still a stash in Chicago," Brett offered, "We could swing by there an' pull the cash before we roll out."

"Yes," she nodded, "That does sound like a good idea."

Finishing their meal, they cleaned up and packed away their gear. "I'll turn in the key," Mason offered. "You guys go hit the storage, and we can meet up at that little diner where we ate."

Outside, Geek opted to ride in the car with Eli, as opposed to riding behind the girl. Arriving at the diner first, they made their way inside, she and Michael right behind them. Choosing a booth alone, she pulled out the folded map to inspect while they waited.

Sliding onto the bench next to her, Michael made small talk, deciding to use their German, "I called and had the plane moved to Denver. It should be there and ready to go when we're ready to leave. How soon do you want me to book us for LA?"

"If the plane is ready to go, there's no need to do it until we attack the rep's hangout. I've never been inside this one.

Actually, I've ever only been inside one, and that's Miami." She was studying the map as she spoke, not wanting to look at him after their night together, and the words she couldn't bring herself to say.

Michael studied her profile for a full minute, before he finally asked, "Are you sure you're ok?"

The air catching in her lungs, she could feel the tears forming in her eyes. *You're such a crybaby;* she chastised herself, not wanting to wipe at them. "I should have told you that I love you," she paused, drawing a ragged breath. "It could have been our last night together, and I couldn't even bring myself to say it."

"You don't have to say it," he offered calmly, "I know that you do. I know that I don't help, teasing you when you do say it."

Lifting her chin, she looked at him, the tear spilling over as she did so; "Really?"

"Yeah, really," he laughed softly, catching the tiny droplet for her and swiping it away. "I want you to stop worrying about this. About us, and about small towns and rock stars, and… everything. I want you to focus on what we have to do. Like you said last night; this is the time where we stand or fold, because this is going to get ugly. We'll worry about all that other stuff when we're done, and you can tell me then."

His smile made her giggle, and she pressed her lips to his without thinking. "I do love you, Michael Anderson," she whispered.

Catching the back of her head with his hand, he only grinned. "Let's lay out the route, shall we?" Nodding, she opened up the map so they both could see, content to work with him side by side while they waited for the others to join them.

Less than an hour later, they had done so, and the group

gathered around the couple for instruction. "We're going straight into Denver from here. Let's head that way, see how far we make it. I have a feeling we will be spending the night in Omaha, which is about half way."

Michael nodded, "I think that's a good plan. You're a good rider, but you're more accustomed to being the passenger. Especially under these harsher conditions."

"Should I ride with you, and leave my bike here?" she queried, "I mean, we have the extra protective gear, since the temperature is dropping."

"That's up to you," he shrugged, "When it gets down to it, we have no idea what's really going to happen. We can make our plan, but in the end having the extra set of wheels may come in handy, good weather or bad."

"You're right," she managed a small grin. "I'll take it, and if we decide later that we don't need it, we can always leave it behind."

Standing, she followed him outside, and the group climbed onto their bikes, Geek still opting to ride in the car with the smallest man of the group. "I never really did like riding on a motorcycle," he joked as they strapped into the front seats. "Besides, it's a hell of a lot warmer in here."

"You were with the Scorpions, and Tori let you go," Eli shared what he knew with the younger man.

"Yeah," Geek nodded. "I joined them, thinking it would be cool, but they only used me. Then they wouldn't let me leave."

"You're lucky they didn't dump your body somewhere," the federal agent chided him.

"Yeah, no kidding," he agreed, twisting his head around to stretch his neck. "Thank God she came along and got me out of there. I would never have guessed she was compassionate, but," he paused, turning to stare out the window, "She's pretty amazing."

"Yes, she is," Eli agreed, focused on following the group on two wheels in front of him.

Outside the vehicle, the bikes formed a line in pairs, Tori and Michael in the front, followed by Brett and Enrique, with Mason bringing up the rear. The air was crisp, whipping in their faces, even wearing their masks and hand coverings, and she could tell the two in the middle were more than a little displeased about it. Stopping at a quick mart, only one-hundred miles down the road, Tori made her way to the bathroom, then met up with the others, who were inspecting and refueling.

Replacing her gloves, she noticed that Enrique was still fighting with his, "You hate riding in the cold, don't you."

"Yeah," he confessed with a brief nod. "We was headed someplace warm when we seen your picture on the cover of that magazine. Been cold ever since." Looking up at her, his brown orbs softened, "It's ok though. I'm glad we're heres with you."

"Yeah, me too," she admitted quietly. "And that's not true," she teased, "We did have ten days in LA. It was warm there!"

He smiled at her laughter, "Yeah. At least we gets to take the plane after this, and we're headin' south after that."

Michael joined them, stretching inside his own gear, "We doing ok over here?"

"I'm not stopping too often, am I?" she shifted the grin to her mate.

"No, baby girl," he replied. "You stop as often as you need to, to warm up or whatever." Reaching up, he slapped the other man on the arm, "We ready, or you guys need a few more minutes?"

"I'm good," Enrique countered, glancing at the girl.

"Me too," she nodded, and they collected the others to be off again, keeping to the pattern, stopping every one-hundred miles or so for necessities and for a break from the rush of cold air.

Shortly before reaching Omaha, they ran into actual snow. They were more than ready to pull in for the night, and made an effort to locate chains for all of them, in case the poor road conditions continued.

"I guess we're not sleeping at a campground tonight," Mason volunteered while they were ordering their dinner at roadside café.

"No," Tori answered flatly, "We get a motel tonight, get warm and have some showers." It might have only been 6 pm, but the sun had set, and the temperatures, which were already unsettling, would be dropping well below freezing. "Why couldn't we have made this little trip in the summer?" she tossed out jokingly, her face sagging with exhaustion.

The group laughed along with her, and the meal passed comfortably enough. Finding their way to a motel, the group only took three rooms, deciding it would be better to stick close together. Tori got into the shower as soon as they were inside, and had fallen asleep before Michael was finished with his. Curling up behind her between the sheets, he held her in his arms, thankful for one more chance to hold her in the darkness.

It's My Call

The following morning, the group got up early and headed out right after breakfast, again making frequent stops all the way to Denver. Once there, Tori bought everyone a new go-phone and they exchanged numbers, saving them into the memory on each device.

"Why are we doing this, exactly?" Geek put forth the question.

Tori smiled, "We may need to get in touch with each other quickly. We won't always be together, and no one will be able to track us or anything because they're brand new." She waved her little phone at him, unconsciously looking over at Eli as she spoke.

"Don't worry," the agent frowned. "I don't think we are a target of anyone outside The Organization. Godfry wants this done, and he's covering for us."

The girl only nodded, then informed them of the next portion of her plan. "We need to park some of the bikes at the airport. There's security there, and it's unlikely they will be disturbed. I'll ride with Michael and park mine. He and I are going to scout the rep's hangout. While we're doing that, you guys need to acquire alternate vehicles for us. We need a van, full-sized. Plus, we need another car, and leave Eli's with the bikes. Then, you can secure us some lodgings for the night. Something along the lines of what we had last night will do."

Following her to their parking spots, Tori shut off her engine and climbed on behind her husband, leaving the other men to work out the logistics of accomplishing their tasks. Going their separate ways, she and Michael made their way across town, arriving at the small bar she knew housed the reps office. "Do they always use bars?" he asked after they parked up the street, and had a look around.

"Not necessarily," her breath frosted as they walked down the sidewalk. "In fact, this is the only one. The other three are different types of businesses; a diner, a pawn shop, and beauty parlor."

"A beauty parlor?" he shot back in surprise. "What the hell kinda mobster uses a beauty parlor for a front?"

"A smart one, I guess," she shrugged. "If I were a cop, looking to shake somebody down, that's the last place that I would hit."

"Agreed," he said as he opened the door, holding it while she made her way inside, then followed, casting his eyes around the smoke filled room. Switching to German, he kept his voice low, "Head to the bar. We'll order drinks and pretend like we're only passing through."

Making her way over to the row of stools, Tori slid onto one and asked for Coors in a bottle for both of them. Taking a seat next to her, Michael leaned over, catching her back belt loop with his thumb and allowing his hand to hang from it. Picking up the frosty bottle, he continued to peer around, his wife watching as he took a swig.

"You're really going to drink that?" she inquired.

"Yeah, why not? It's only one," he stared at her, aware that she had never seen him touch so much as a drop. "I can hold my liquor, thanks," he gave her a boyish grin.

Leaning against him, she folded her hands and lay still, her eyes searching down the dark hallway that lay on the opposite side of the room, where the shop owners conduced business. "I count six men," she spoke only loud enough for him to hear.

"Yeah, me too," he nonchalantly traded his half empty bottle for her full one. "Pretend to have a drink, love." Sitting up, she obeyed, lifting the brew, but not actually swallowing.

Replacing the glass container on the bar, she announced her potty break and headed for the bathroom. Making her way down the other hallway, part of the public areas of the bar, she peeked into the open doors as she made her way by. Taking care of her business, she exited a few minutes later, noticing that there were a few more men in the room than before.

Arriving back at her husband, he turned, allowing her to stand between his legs as he grinned at her, and she leaned forward to kiss him, feeling her stomach turn at the taste of him. Sensing her distress, he looped his arm around her, "You ok?"

Shaking her head, "Why does everyone keep asking me that?" she muttered, then called out rather loudly, "I don't feel well. Kinda dizzy. You mind calling it an early night?"

"Naw, baby," he gave her a small squeeze and pulled out his wallet to drop a $20 on the bar. "Thanks," he gave the bartender a nod and led her back out, into the cold.

"Are you really sick?" he asked as they arrived at his bike.

"A little," she confessed, pulling on her gloves. "I should call Eli and find out where we're staying." Flipping open her phone, she discovered that he had sent her a text, containing directions to their motel, a room number, and a little smiley face, which made her giggle.

"What?" Michael swung onto the leather seat, and she showed him the message. "Awww, isn't that sweet. I think he still likes you," he cooed.

Tori grimaced. "Yeah, he does. Not that it means

anything," she replied, then swung herself onto the seat behind him, thankful she hadn't ridden over on her own.

Arriving at the rooms a short time later, they discovered that they were the last ones there. Knocking on the door that Eli had indicated, they were allowed to make their way inside, only to discover it would be, in fact, their only room.

Seeing her displeased scowl, he explained, "Something's going on in town, and there're no rooms, anywhere. I was lucky to get this one."

"It's ok; we can share. It's not like the floor is harder than the ground," her mate quipped easily; seeing Enrique grinning, he corrected, "The beds, buddy… we can share the beds."

"Right," the other man nodded in an exaggerated fashion. "Yeah, I guess we've pretty much settled the other 'sharing,' haven' we, baby girl." He grabbed her, turning her and pressing the front of his body against hers, leaning in and breathing into her ear.

"I'm really tired, baby," she leaned her forehead against his, curious if her husband would react. To her surprise, the action didn't have the effect she had anticipated. Instead, her mate turned his back, grunting while he dug through his bag for something, basically ignoring them. The rest of the group stared at the trio, their odd behavior too commonplace to worry over.

Enrique's arms around her, his hands moved up her back, "Its ok," he conceded, seeing that he wasn't going to get a rise out of the other man. "You get some sleep, baby girl. No one's gonna bothers you." His fingers ran through her tresses, and he gave her a small peck on her cheek before he released her.

Pushing past him to stand between the two beds, Tori pulled off her boots and dropped her jeans to the floor. Unhooking her bra, she slid it out through an armhole, and it landed on top of the denim. Finally, she climbed into the bed on her left, wearing only her tee and panties. "I don't care who sleeps with me, just don't wake me up," she called out as she scrunched into the center of the bed, taking one of the pillows for herself.

The room was dead quiet, as pairs of eyes flicked from one man to the next. Finally, Brett spoke up, "Part o' us can take the floor. It's really not a big deal," his mind briefly contemplating if she weren't in her current condition, would the group actually share her?

Assuming sleeping positions, Michael stripped down to his briefs and slid into the bed behind his wife. Draping his arm across her, he breathed into her hair, allowing his hand to push its way down to rest on the lower part of her stomach. *Things are changing fast, love. We have to make it through this. All of us.* Closing his eyes, he also drifted off to sleep.

Black as Night

The following morning, they took turns in the shower, getting dressed and then making their way to a café for coffee before they split up. Michael, Tori and Enrique occupied the van, going to pick up the supplies from the storage, while the others took the remaining bikes over to the airport to park them.

They regrouped two hours later a few blocks from the bar, at another diner. Pushing a few tables together, they made their final plans, and waited for the right moment to make their move.

"Are you sure this's the plan you want to follow?" Michael asked after they were seated.

"Of course, it is," she glared at him with tired eyes, "Why do you ask?"

"Because, if you've had a change of heart, or have decided on a different path, now's the time to speak up. Otherwise, once we leave here, there's no turning back." He paused, giving her a moment to decide, and then pushed on, "I'll call and have the plane ready. We hit these guys before the bar opens, and clean them out."

"They all die," she muttered, sipping from her glass of water.

"Yeah," he exhaled noisily through his nose, suddenly not sure he was prepared to watch his wife take a man's life. "That's what I meant. Anyways, we get to the airport, maybe an hour, hopefully, less. This isn't one of our usual places, so it may take a while. From there, about two hours to LA."

"Yup," Tori flicked her eyes up at him, "And I'll give you further directions on the plane. When we get there, we want the turnaround time to be as short as possible." She looked dolefully at the group, her mood somber. Watching the elderly man who wiped down the counter, her mind drifted away, to a diner in Texas, where Trish spent her days, working to build a future and provide for her sons.

"This won't be as easy as I thought it would be," she confessed, her voice low.

"You don't thinks we can do this?" Enrique sounded miffed.

"No, that's not it. When I was pissed about them hurting my family, or my friends, I wanted this badly, but if they're not in any danger, things are less... clear." Her shoulders had slowly been sinking into a droop; her thoughts still muddled.

"That's what I was talking about," Michael pointed at his bride for a moment, then retracted the digit. "We could skip all of this, go straight down and cut off the head. I think that would be much cleaner."

"No, this is the plan we should follow," she nodded, still watching the shop's owner, "I'm sure of it."

Another patron entered the café, taking a seat at the counter on one of the polished stools. The old man glanced over at him, not bothering to ask for his order. Instead, he went into the back, returning shortly with an envelope, which the man placed inside his jacket, in an inner pocket.

"You were short last week," the patron's voice was gruff, his Spanish a little less than smooth.

"Yes, sir," the old man picked up his rag to wring it between his hands, "Better business, better pay," he replied in broken English.

Tori stiffened, grinding her teeth as she listened. Enrique, seated next to her, stretched his arm behind her, toying with her hair as he studied her placid features.

"Relax, baby girl. We gots this," he leaned closer to her to whisper, and her stomach did a summersault when she met his gaze.

"I know, baby," she murmured back, returning her focus to the shop's owner.

Watching the patron depart a few minutes later, her blood began to boil. Flicking her eyes over at the victim, she could see the fear on his face, and she knew what the envelope contained. Standing, she called to the others, "Let's go. Eli, you and Geek bring the vehicles, but hang back and follow."

Outside, the patron walked, and she could hear him whistling as he entered a shop a few doors down.

"What're you going to do?" Michael interrupted her thoughts.

"Well, I'm not going to cut off the head," she moved a few steps closer to wait, her eyes roaming the street. "I'm going to break their fucking backs." The man exited a few minutes later, continuing down the walk, and she matched his pace, the rest of the group falling in behind after she had gotten a good lead.

With the number of people coming and going, the patron turned the corner, unaware of being followed. Tori cursed him as they moved, *sorry bastards; taking from people who work so hard*. If she had needed reminding why she had agreed to this job, he had done well. She wouldn't do this for herself; this would be for all the people that they hurt.

Quickening her pace, she caught up to the man, measuring him to be about her height, with broad shoulders beneath the heavy coat. Right on his heels, he cut through the alley, headed for the bar.

Catching him with a blow to the back of the neck, she knocked him to the ground.

He rolled, getting to his feet, and spinning around to face her. Seeing his assailant, he released a boisterous laugh, "What the fuck're you up to, bitch?" dusting snow from his jacket.

"I'd like an introduction," she stated calmly, staring with steely grey eyes.

Laughing even louder, he glared at her team as they came up behind her, "These guys with you?" he tossed his chin at them.

"Yeah, this's my crew," she appeared unruffled.

"*Your* crew," he wiped his nose with the back of his glove, "Bitches don't run crews. You must have the wrong guy," he sneered.

"You work for The Organization, yes?"

His mouth hung open slightly, "Some days," he nodded, peering past her again at the men behind her. Taking a moment, he appeared to be weighing his options. "This way," he finally waved for her to follow, "But if they don't accept you, you'll leave in a body bag," he warned.

"I'll take my chances," she walked beside him, keeping her gaze moving and watching for trouble.

Entering the bar, the man called out immediately, "Hey, Hector! Some broad here to see you." Turning to look at her over his shoulder, he smirked, pulling off his gloves.

Hector turned out to be a rather short for a man, five-foot eight at best. Coming out from the business side of the bar, he held a pistol in his hand, wiping it down with a rag. "Some broad, huh," he grinned at the girl, looking her up and down. "You's here las' night. I seen you."

"I was," she smiled crookedly.

"And what's it you wants?" his eyes flicked down at the gun he was holding, watching her move calmly around his showroom, picking up a pool cue and turning it in her hands.

Eight men, gangs all here, she counted mentally. "I want

to know how to find the Spiders. Where are they?" she asked aloud, twisting her stick. She looked away, hearing the rumble begin low and build from several of their opponents.

"Spiders? What spiders?" he challenged her with a sneer, shoving his chest out for display, toying with her.

"The ones you command," she didn't mince words, "When The Organization sends word... I'm sure they're pretty busy as of late."

His smile disappeared, "You got some set o' balls, for a bitch... comin' in heres askin' 'bout 'em by name."

Her eyes swept over to stare at him, squinting slightly. "That's cause I ain't scared o' them," she drawled, "Now, we gots sum choices here. You tell me where they's at, or I can beats the shit outta ya, an' then ya can tells me."

He full on laughed in response. "Ya hear this bitch?" he bellowed. "Thinks she's a badass." He popped the rag, rocking his jaw for a moment, "Kills 'em."

His lackeys leapt into action, Tori catching the one coming for her upside the head, then her knife popped open while he spun around. The next instant, it found its way between his ribs, piercing his heart before she pulled it free. With a quick side step, she caught the one that Michael battled in the back of the head with the cue, then slit his throat cleanly from behind. Thirty seconds in, Hector and the patron were the only two left alive.

"Hold him," she commanded, pointing at the larger man, flicking her knife in her right hand and clutching her makeshift club in the other. Turning to face the leader, she could tell by the look on his face that the gun was empty.

"Now, Hector; I can see that you're a smart man," she worked her way up to him, backing him against the wall. "Little men don't get to be lead, unless they're smart," she mocked him as she spoke.

"Who are you?" his voice jumped a few levels, no longer

deep enough to pass for a man.

"I'm death," she breathed, close enough to touch him, glaring down at his wide brown eyes. "That your second?" she tossed her head at the man her colleagues had on his knees, flanking him, while she slipped the knife into her pocket.

"No," he bit at her. "They're gonna kill you. Nobody fucks with them."

"Who?" she laughed in a low tone, "The Organization? I told you, I ain't sceered o' them," she punched him in the sternum with the heel of her hand, "Tell me where the Spiders are!"

"You go's to hell!"

"Break his legs," she bade over her shoulder.

Immediately, Michael swung his pool cue, catching the patron in the face and knocking him over, his legs sprawling. Taking full swings with the heavy end of the stick, her mate crushed his knee caps, the cracking noise quickly followed by howls of pain.

Hector's eyes grew wide at the scene, "You're crazy, bitch!"

Tori tossed the cue into her right hand, smashing it against the edge of pool table next to her, causing it to break off into a long, sharp point with the grain of the wood. Pinning the man before her against the wall, she dug the tip of her modified weapon into the hollow of his neck, "Crazy is only the beginning. You should talk, while you still can."

"I can't tells you shit, lady! You know what they do to people who talk? To their families?"

"Yeah, I know! Trust me," her voice loud, her lips curled with rage, "You got about ten seconds, and then I'm not gonna wait anymore!"

"You go's to hell, cunt!" he clenched his jaw, ready for the end.

"I'll see you there," she breathed, shoving the stick through his jugular and into his windpipe.

Michael stared, transfixed by the ease with which she had moved, pulling the wood free and listening to the gurgling of Hector's last breath as it escaped through the new hole. Moving out of her way when she spun around, he watched while she dropped onto the patron's belly. Spinning the weapon so she could wave the fat end like a club, her eyes were black as night.

"I'll talk! I'll talk!" her victim screamed.

"The fuck if you will," her voice flat calm, her hand swung time and again, until his cranium had been reduced to mush. Rising, she didn't look at her group mates, "Get the drill. We clean out the file cabinet." Making her way to the back, she pulled out the key, testing it on the small grey box to discover it didn't work.

Mason came in, carrying the tool, "Here. Let me at it."

Moving out of the way, Tori began to clean the blood splatter from her face in Hector's private bathroom. "Watch the door. Anyone comes in, kill them," she commanded, and Enrique moved to comply. "Is the plane ready?" she addressed her husband, while removing her jacket to inspect it.

"Yes," he replied coolly, "I made the call while we were following the collector."

"Good," she glanced up at him, "You did well, by the way. Wasn't sure you would really have it in you."

"Yeah," his breath was a little heavy. "I was thinking the same thing about you. Enrique's not the only one with a dark side," he flickered a grin, their eyes locked for a moment, and their connection had never been stronger.

"I got it!" Mason hollered, pulling the top drawer open to reveal a few stacks of cash and a green, hard bound book.

"Leave the money," Tori interjected, snatching up the log

and closing the drawer to peek in the bottom one, which held stacks of similar notebooks. Closing it, she called out calmly, "Let's go," taking the single volume with her.

"That's it?" Brett followed, speaking up in disgust, "You're not gonna look around or nothin'?"

"No," she stated flatly, "This is what we came for. That, and the bodies. Keep a count for me. I'd like to know how many we got by the end."

Climbing into the van, the men appeared unruffled. "Go straight to the airport. Take nothing from the van; no weapons of any kind. Do not park anywhere near the bikes. Eli and I will meet you at the plane." Slamming the door shut, she turned and walked up the block, climbing into the beat up sedan, "Why did you pick such a rough looking vehicle?" she inquired smoothly.

"You didn't specify, so I tried to economize," he grinned at her, "How did it go?"

"It went," her voice gave nothing away. "Get us to the plane, Eli. I'm going to need you to get me through security. And you need to call Godfry, immediately. Inform him that the bar is soaked in blood, and there's a shit ton of materials in their office that will need to be secured."

"Yes, ma'am," he pulled out his regular cell to make the call.

Only half listening to his end of the conversation, Tori cracked open the book she had taken, inspecting the first few pages. A ledger, it contained dates and some sort of code. *Damn.* Of course, she knew it had been smart, as even if it fell into the wrong hands, it would be unreadable to anyone outside of The Organization.

Hearing his device snap shut, she looked over at him, "Well?"

"He's sending a team to the bar, and he'll make a call to the airport. You're in my custody, so when we get there, I will present my badge, and you keep your mouth shut." He grinned at her, happy to be useful in their endeavor. "Give me your weapons, and I'll carry them for you."

"Of course," she peered out the window, seeing that they were already at the gate to the parking area. "Don't park close to the others. They can message us with their phones if they have any trouble. Otherwise, we spread out." She pulled out her nine, and both switchblades to hand to him.

"I see," he agreed, easing into a parking space, placing his claim ticket in the window. Taking the weapons, he could not resist, "Two knives?"

Tori grinned, "What can I say?" and climbed out of the car.

Fifteen minutes later, everyone had boarded their transport, the pass through security running like clockwork. Sinking into a chair, Tori placed her face in her hands and breathed deeply. Taking a seat next to her, Michael rested his hand on her shoulder, "How are you?"

She breathed through her fingers. "I'm tired, love. Just tired."

All taking seats, they waited for takeoff; when they had leveled out, the girl presented them with their next set of chores. "That went pretty smoothly," she praised, "I hope we can keep up the momentum."

Mason studied her as she spoke, "I have to hand it to you, you're even better than I had realized. And you are definitely a cold hearted bitch."

"Thanks," she tossed back at him, "I learned from the best." Her briefing completed a few minutes later; she turned to the window, closing her eyes and crashing for what sleep she could get before they moved on their next target.

Yesterday's Prize

Arriving in LA, the group set about their task of renting a van and a car to work from. Tori had noted the time, informing them that she wanted to be back on the plane by 5:00 pm, Denver time, so they had less than three hours to get the job done. Again, they split up to make things go quicker, and reconvened at the pawn shop, having been instructed to go inside and look around as if they were shopping until everyone had arrived.

Tori, Michael and Enrique arrived last, and she noted that her group had done exactly as they were instructed. Seeing them enter, Eli and Geek exited to wait in the vehicles, ready to leave or to warn them of any trouble. Making her way to the glass counter in the back, the girl cracked her knuckles, ready to begin.

"Hi," she smiled brightly at the balding man before her, "I'm here for something… special."

"Ok, whatcha got in mind?" he didn't return her grin.

"Well, aren't you friendly," she mocked him, showing fewer teeth.

He stared at her, clenching his jaw. His eyes shifted to peer behind her for a brief instant, and she knew someone had come up behind her. Looking at the front of the glass, she made out her mate.

"Something's wrong," she called to him in German. As soon as she spoke, the man swung around, reaching for a weapon as far as she could tell. Leaping over the case, she caught him in the back and knocked him to the ground, slitting his throat and allowing his head to hit the carpet with a thud.

"Lock the doors!" she called to her team, "And close the blinds… shut off that *open* sign. That's it." Moving quickly, she determined that they were alone in the front. "Enrique, call out if anyone comes inside with a key," she wafted her hand at the others, indicating for them to follow her down the hall to the back.

Pulling her 9-mm pistol out, she switched the safety off. Holding it up in front of her, she slid along the wall. Nearing the end, she could hear music and voices coming from the last room.

Waving to the others, they positioned themselves against the sides as well, and she called into the room, hiding her gun next to her thigh, "Anybody home?" Seeing a man move, she returned the pistol to its hiding place and stepped into the door frame.

"Hey," she called lightly, "There's no one out front." From her vantage point, she could see there were only two others. "Hello, fellas," she nodded at them.

The man ambled towards her, quite large and wearing a Hawaiian shirt that reminded her briefly of Terry. The room being well lit, and the hallway dark, she knew he would be blind when he passed the threshold. Allowing him to move past her, into the reach of her companions, she darted into the room, redrawing her weapon and shoving it into one of the two other men's faces. "Don't move!" she commanded.

Waiting for the chaos in the passage to die down, no shots rang out, and a minute later, the fat man lay face down on the floor with his blood oozing out onto the tile. "Clear!" her husband's voice called to her, causing her to grin.

"Well," she sneered at her prisoners, "Our last stop

proved somewhat fruitless. Perhaps you gentlemen will be a bit more cooperative." She kept them covered, while her friends joined them, securing their hands behind their backs with zip-ties. She then snapped the safety on and tucked the pistol into the small of her back.

"What do you want?" the older of the two inquired.

"Spiders," she replied softly, her eyes looking around the room, taking in the furnishings and locating the filing cabinet. "I'm looking for the Spiders." Toying with him, she smiled coyly, "You wouldn't happen to know where they are?"

The silver-haired gent remained calm, his crinkled brown face giving nothing away. "I'm sure you will find them eventually. Or they will find you."

Tori held her grin, aware that he knew who she was. "How long ago did you send them out? How many days?"

"Not enough," he replied. "You had already left town by the time I got them the orders." He inhaled deeply, "I have to admit, I'm very surprised you would return. I figured you ran… at least that's what you should have done."

"Naw," her smile morphed into something darker, "Hiding was yesterday's prize. Today, I want something more." She slowly paced around the room to have a look at what lay on top of the desk, stalling. "I guess there's nothing more you would be willing to tell me?"

"A thousand platitudes leap into my brain," he chuckled, "And not one of them will save you."

"I don't wanna be saved," she cut her eyes over at him, her hand tracing the edge of the desk, "I wanna be avenged. I wanna rain down pain and wreak havoc on The Organization." She paused, watching him swallow with tightly drawn lips, "Does that bother you?"

She stared at him, briefly waiting for a reply. "You must be a weak little man, hiding in this office and ordering the deaths of others. Where's the rest of your men? You can't tell me the four of you is all that there are."

At that moment, Enrique was at the door; "Keys."

With a flash, Tori popped open her knife, killing the silver-haired gentleman before he could utter a sound, wiping his blood on his lapel. Turning to the other, she held her finger to her lips, breathing a soft, "Sshhhh," then she moved to the door and slipped down the hall, Enrique close behind her.

Michael remained in the room, staring at the younger man, hardly more than a boy. Pulling out a revolver, he cocked it, waiting for whatever would come next.

A few minutes later, the pair of them returned, "All clear," she breathed with a giggle, running her hand across her husband's chest. "They had gone to get something to eat and just let themselves in, like dumbasses."

Looking up at her, the boy stammered, "Are they dead?"

"Of course they're dead," she kneeled down in front of him. "You got a name, little man?"

He stared at her, his brown eyes as big as saucers, "Juan."

"Hi, Juan," she breathed. "I'm Tori. I would shake your hand, but you're not really in a position for that." She smiled at him, cocking her head slightly to the side to gaze up at him. "I'm curious, Juan. What're you doing here?"

"Learning," his voice quivered. "I'm here to learn."

"You're in training, huh? You're awfully young to be in the back. I thought back rooms were only for seasoned veterans."

He nodded, "Grandpa was teaching me the business. To take his place."

"That was your Grandpa?" she indicated the body in the chair next to his.

"Yes," his head bobbed, his jaw tight with rage.

Tori pursed her lips, "Wow, that must suck, watching him die like that." She waited to see if he would cry; when he didn't she continued, "You have any other family, Juan?"

"No," he began to shake his head in wide sweeps, the tears finally spilling over and running down his cheek.

"Awww," she cooed, reaching out to squeeze his leg. "Don't worry, Juan. I'm not gonna hurt your family. I only hurt bad people. People who deserve to be… hurt."

Michael shifted his stance behind her, growing impatient.

"How's our time?" she asked towards the floor between them.

"Short," her mate chirped.

Turning her attention back to the boy, she smiled again, "Where did the Spiders go, Juan?"

"I can't tell you that," he shook his head, more tears streaming down his smooth face.

"You're going to make me angry, Juan. You see what I did to Grandpa?" she nodded to encourage him. "I wasn't angry when I did that, Juan."

His orbs moved over to the side, so that he could see the body slumped next to him, the blood beginning to pool on the floor around their chairs. "He was a good man," he huffed.

Tori rolled her eyes, standing in front of the young man and grabbing his jaw, jerking him so that he was looking at her again.

"Shut up, Juan! Your grandfather was a murderer! A horrible man in a horrible world filled with thieves and abusers! He got what he deserved, Juan!" She sensed her companions growing tense at her tirade, but they held their tongues.

Tightening her grip on his soft flesh, she could feel his teeth below the skin as she squeezed. Grinding her own, she wanted to punish him for making her work so hard. Her chest

131

heaved noticeably; she opened her hand, releasing his face, holding it up so that he could see it suspended above him. "It's a shame that I killed him first. I think I might have gotten a little more for my effort if I had let him watch you die."

He stared at her, snot dripping from his nose, "You're an evil woman."

Glaring at him, she convulsed, resisting the urge to giggle; resisting and losing as the cackle started low, building into a rolling laugh. "I'm evil." Turning her back on him, she waved an open palm at her mate, "I'm evil, he says; did you hear that?"

Michael watched her, his discomfort with her performance growing by the minute.

"I warned you, love," she hissed. Popping her knife out, she swung around to the boy, placing the blade at his throat, so that the point dimpled the delicate skin, her voice a loud whisper. "I am evil, Juan. I am because they made me so. This world, these people you are protecting. They raised me; they created me, to be… evil… for them."

"We have two paths we can take, Juan. You can come with me, on the path that leads to a different life, but to make it, we must destroy the other one, the old life. Are you on the old path, Juan? Come with me, Juan… take the new path… tell me where he sent the Spiders… Leave the old path and let it die."

She leaned over him, pushing the knife against him so hard that his head lay back enough to stare at the ceiling straight above him, a trickle of blood beginning to run down his stretched neck.

"I don't know the name of it. I swear to you; I don't know where," he paused, daring to swallow, "They were going to find you… at home."

Tori's jaw dropped, her gut wrenching in agony,

"Home…"

"Oh, dear God," Michael's voice cut through her pain, "Come on, baby girl; we gotta go, now!"

Releasing the boy, she flipped open her phone. She called Eli, who would still be waiting out front, demanding as soon as he said hello, "Get Godfry; they are going after my family. I have a boy in here, alive; I'm leaving him tied up, so they will need to get here ASAP."

Not waiting for a reply, she snapped the device shut. Waving her hand at Mason, she indicated they needed to open the drawers, and he bolted for the front door, ready to retrieve their tools. Running her trembling fingers through her hair, she stared at the floor and waited.

Her accomplice returned quickly, inquiring if she had tried the key. Handing it to him, he attempted it first, then drilled the lock. Once again, they found stacks of cash, along with a hard bound log book, which she took. Turning to the boy, she knelt down in front of him, her lips forming the faintest of smiles.

"Thank you, Juan," her pink lips breathed. "I'm not sure what the Feds will do with you, but I truly hope you find a better path." Standing quickly, she glanced around, exiting the room with the rest of her crew in tow.

Cat and Mouse

Inside the van, Michael moved to call the airport. Stopping him, Tori inquired, "Where're we going?"

"To San Antonio, of course," he bit sharply, "We have to get home."

"That isn't the home they are going to," she replied softly.

"What're you talking about," he stammered. "The boy said they were going to catch you at home."

"That's right," she breathed, "Catch *me*. We have given no indication that we went to Texas. I still have Danny's phone, so that fingerprint is still there as well, if they look. I believe they will try to get to me at the house in Florida, but more likely the house in New Jersey."

"And what makes you think that?"

"Because I'm going to lead them there," she smiled, pulling out her brother's cell. "Call the airport, and get us the flight to Florida next. We still need to take out the Miami office. I'm going to ask Collin to help us set a trap." Her husband stared at her for a moment, before pushing the buttons to make the call.

Using Brian's device, Tori reached Collin, greeting him warmly, "Hey, honey; how are you?"

"Uhh; hi, Tori. What's up?" he sounded confused.

"It's time to kiss and make up, hun. I need you to put out the word that we've reconciled our differences, and that we are throwing a huge bash there at the New Jersey mansion in three days. Set it up however you normally would – caterers, open bar, whatever. Really sell it. We want everything delivered, and tell them we will serve it ourselves."

"Anyone in particular you want to invite?" he sounded a bit miffed at being ordered around by the girl.

"Haha, no, I don't really want any guests. The ones I need will be crashing the party," she laughed to herself in earnest.

"And once again, you've lost me. You are definitely a freak of society, but I'll do it. Is Brian going to be here?" his voice dropped at the end.

"Brian is fine, hun. Set up the party, and expect him to return. He's not mad at you guys, and I assume eventually, this will all work out and we'll play together again. I can't give you any more than that. Please be ready for us," she smiled, aware that on some level she did really want her chance to be in the band and to go on the tour.

The group made it onto the plane without issues, taking their seats and settling in for the long flight to Florida, their second time in a week to do so. With the plane in the air, her husband couldn't hold his questions any longer.

"You are deviating from the plan, and I want to know how and why," his spat at her, anger adding an edge to his words.

"I don't understand why you're upset," she replied calmly.

"Why I'm upset? I just watched you torture some kid, who might have been twenty years old, and was still wet behind the ears, and then you are ignoring what he told you?" his face flushed, Tori felt taken aback by his torrent.

"I see; I guess you would've rather I tortured the old man," she gazed out the window, collecting her thoughts. "I did what was necessary to get the information I needed from him. And yes, I was panicked when I heard his words as well. But, I quickly realized, this could work to our advantage."

"And how's that?" Mason cut in, equally disturbed by what he'd seen. "You have no morals, Tori. I honestly think that you and Enrique were made for each other," he tossed his chin at the other man, clenching his jaw in disgust.

She chuckled, flicking her gaze at her former lover to see he grinned from ear to ear, "Yes, he and I do share a bit of a dark streak," she admitted quietly. "However, that's not all there is to me."

Shaking her black waves, she stared into the sky to her right, turning her plan in her mind, checking it for faults. Finding none, she shared; "We still need to eliminate the branches in Miami and New York. That will insure that the Spiders will be cut off from The Organization. They will only be able to act on their last given order, which was to attack *me*," she poked her chest to emphasize the word *me*.

"Of course, that does not guarantee that they will do so, but I feel strongly that they will." She pulled her gaze away from the view, taking in the faces of her crew. "I'm having Collin organize a huge party at the house; a fake one. It'll give them a location of where I will be; a glowing opportunity for them to make their move."

"A trap," Enrique blurted, "Like we wanted to set; only using your friends as bait."

"Exactly," she nodded, "A trap. And my friends will be fine. When they show up, there won't be any surprise; we will be expecting them. We will deal with them accordingly, and then move on to take out Rico and Ruben Ramirez, in El Paso. And because we will have cut the legs out from under them, we won't have to rush or worry about them getting support."

Michael stared at his bride, speechless in his awe. "That's

136

fucking brilliant," he finally admitted. "Unless they run and hide."

"They can't hide," she stated flatly. "We've identified them. And in this day and age, it's virtually impossible to be completely untraceable." She nodded at Eli, giving him a small smile, "One way, or another, we will get them, like a game of cat and mouse." Turning back to her window, she lay her head against the glass and fell asleep, leaving the men to discuss the turn of events without her.

Classic

Reaching MIA early the following morning, the group had become practiced at what would be expected of them. Breaking up into the proper subunits, they met up at the designated coffee shop at the tail end of breakfast, prepared for their briefing in a completely relaxed state.

"This is going to be a little different," the girl explained, sipping on a cup of black coffee while the men enjoyed their breakfast. "This office is housed in the back of a beauty parlor. If you look out that side window," she indicated with an extended pinkie, "You can see the glass front to the building I'm talking about."

"Yeah, you told me about this one," Michael grinned between bites. "Their creative thinking makes it almost classic."

Brett nodded his agreement, recalling all the times he had visited the place. "We go in through th' back, o' course," he supplied, "As the front is typically filled with blue haired ol' biddies, getting their weekly primp session." He cut his eyes over at the dark haired beauty seated across from him, "Makes a man appreciate the simpler kind o' girl; now *that's* a classic," he offered his cup in a toast.

Tori flushed at the compliment, "Thanks, Brett." Her eyes darting over to her mate, she struggled to remain focused on the necessities, "He's right, we go in through the back. Of course, I have a plan for clearing out the old ladies, in case things get ugly, if Geek would be able to pull it off."

Looking up in surprise, the youngest member of their group grinned, "You mean you have something I can do, besides driving the van?"

"Maybe," she teased. "I'd like to put them in the dark."

He laughed at the phrase, "Ok, the whole building, or only the front?"

"Preferably only the front. They won't be able to do much primping without power. You think you can make that happen?" she sneered at her devious plan that would surely keep the number of innocents in the building to a minimum.

"Sure," Geek shrugged. "They have Wi-Fi here, let me get my laptop, and I'll see what I can come up with." Leaving the group, he went to the van to retrieve his gear. Returning a few minutes later, he set up his machine in a booth and began to poke around in that wonderful world of cyberspace, researching his options with a small, elated grin.

"What if he's not able to run them out?" Michael asked in a low voice, "We still hit this one?"

"Oh yeah," Tori replied, "The office is in the back. This is the one that I have been inside the reps quarters before; the only one." She smiled at Brett, recalling the time she had played his second. "That was the meeting that led to the downfall of the Scorpions."

"Don' remind me," the red-headed man teased.

"Anyways, the two areas are connected, but operate independently of each other. Either way, Enrique takes the door that goes between the office and the front, and hopefully we won't have any issues. We also don't want any gunfire if we can help it, as we only have the one silenced weapon. Mason, I'm going to have you carrying that one."

Hunt nodded his understanding, while holding a straight face.

"Other than that, it's pretty much the same routine. We

have what we need to know about the Spiders, so this is a straight up hit. Everybody dies," she finished in a low voice, her eyes darting around, noting that the place was pretty deserted.

"I'm glad I always get the easy jobs," Eli teased. "Sitting in the car is almost more excitement than I can handle."

"You say that now," she tossed her hair. "But if the shit were to hit the fan, your job would suddenly become the most important; getting us the hell out of there – you and Geek." She smiled at the young man who had rejoined the group, "We ready?"

"Easy money," he winked at her. "They're down, and will be for a few hours, unless someone figures out what I did and undoes it."

"Jesus Christ," Enrique slapped the table, "You can knocks out their power, that easy?"

"Well, you know, they don't call me Geek for no reason," he leaned back in his chair, savoring the praise.

"That's good," Tori redirected the conversation, "We give them about twenty minutes to clear out, and then we can move. For the time being, I'm going to the ladies' room."

"She still doesn't know?" Eli asked quietly after she left the group.

"I don't think so," Michael replied, lifting his cup. "She's still exhibiting the symptoms, but without an actual test, I can't say for sure. If we get this wrapped up in time, she may still make her appointment with that doctor of hers. We'll know more then."

Hitting the building on schedule, they were in and out in under ten minutes, wiping out the entire crew easily, with zero collateral damage. Eli made the call to Godfry on the way to the airport, relieved to report how smoothly things had run.

Their luck held, and the New York rep went down even

more easily, being housed in a diner. Arriving there in late evening, the group camped out until the place had cleared of extraneous patrons, then wiped the joint and walked away. Checking into a hotel to get some real rest, the group would be ready to make their way to the house in New Jersey for the party the following night.

How the Cookie Crumbles

Tori awoke early the following day, darting for the bathroom and heaving her guts up, *every fucking morning seems like; and I didn't even eat yet.* Drifting off to sleep the night before, a sickening thought had occurred to her as to why Michael had taken her pills from her and hidden them. *My God, if I'm pregnant,* she sniffed, *this isn't the time for this.* Still leaning over the sink when he joined her, she decided to clear the air.

"You *would* tell me, wouldn't you?" she inquired softly, staring at his reflection beside her.

"Tell you what?" his brow raised slightly.

Standing up straight, she turned to look him in the eye, "I'm not sick, am I," she breathed, only inches from him.

"Hmmm," he reached up to catch her arms, giving her biceps a firm squeeze, staring at her lips. "You know, sometimes, things happen, and there is no plan. Sometimes, it's just how the cookie crumbles. At the moment, we have things we have to deal with, and we can't let this interfere. We take care of business, and then we can go home, and you can see your doctor."

He lifted his gaze, taking in her crystal blue eyes, "I didn't want to say anything, love. I didn't want to break your focus since there's really nothing we can do at this point. I'm sorry."

"You're sure then," she breathed, fighting the panic.

"The doctor said it could make things worse."

"Hey!" he raised his voice slightly, "Don't worry about that. It is what it is. If you are, if you're not, whatever or however things turn out. We can't worry about it right this minute. We need clear heads here, end of story."

Tori nodded her understanding, sliding her fingers up his bare arms and around his neck to hold him against her. "Are you mad?"

"No, love, I'm not mad." Tightening his grip, he nuzzled her ear, "Put it out of your head. I don't want to talk about it again until this is over, ok?"

"Ok," she agreed softly. "I can do that," she gave him a weak smile, wiping at her moist cheek. "At least now I know why I feel like shit all the time," she grimaced.

"Yeah," he smiled briefly, "So don't take it so hard. Get dressed, and let's get downstairs. We need to get over to the house and set up for the party tonight, and the guests of honor."

"Right," she agreed, moving to comply, not bothering to ask if the rest of the guys knew; she felt fairly certain she had been the last one in on the secret.

Arriving at the estate by late-morning, Tori noticed that the group had become a cohesive unit, with every member valued and accepted. Smiling to herself, she wondered what would become of them after their task had been completed, and if they would remain friends; she hoped that they would.

At the front door, she reached for the handle and finding it unlocked, let herself in. "I think there's a bedroom unoccupied that Eli and Geek can share," she informed them in the foyer. "Of course, Chuck's old room is also empty, which I think should go to Mason."

"Why do we have to share?" Eli and Geek protested almost on top of each other.

"Because I said so," she replied, climbing the stairs to her own room for a few moments of rest. Soon, she would need to meet with Collin to go over the evening's plans, but it could wait. Dropping her pack on the floor of the closet, she kicked off her boots and stretched onto her belly, happy to be home, or at least in her own room and on her own bed.

To her surprise, she awoke to find her husband staring at her, waiting for her nap to end as patiently as he could muster.

"Hey," he said quietly, his hand moving to run down the length of her back, "We have a problem."

Pushing up onto her elbow, she scowled, "What kind of problem? Did they not arrange for the party? It's very public, I hope."

"Yes," he maintained his outward composure, "The party is set, and you guys made the tabloids, so everyone knows that *Indelible* is back on again." He hesitated, hating to be the bearer of bad news, "Actually, we have two problems, the first one, he invited actual guests, and the other two bands from the tour are coming. As for the second... Brian and Lindsey are downstairs."

"Holy fuck!" she screamed, "What the hell do you mean they're downstairs!?!" she struggled to sit up on the pliable surface.

"Sshsshssh," he hissed, trying to calm her. "There's no use being upset. He saw an article yesterday that you guys were getting back together, and they jumped on a plane."

"Jesus Christ!" she ran her fingers through her hair, "Does he have any idea how this complicates things?" deep lines marked her face. "And did you say they invited actual guests?"

"Yes; he thought it would make things look more convincing. It's only about a dozen people or so, if they bring dates, but we'll have to decide what to do with them. You know things have the potential to get ugly," he surprised himself at his ability to maintain his self-control, considering the fit he had thrown while she slept.

"Oh my God," she pressed her face into her hands, leaning forward to stretch her back. "Can we have one thing in this whole damn operation run smoothly?"

"I know you're upset, and you have every right to be. But it's not going to help, and if it makes you feel any better, I gave both of them what for while you were resting. They know they fucked up, so there's no need in you getting all worked up about it."

"Ok," she agreed. "I promise I won't throw a tantrum," she reached over to rest her hand on his chest. "And I appreciate you looking out for me. I guess you've been doing it for a while, and I didn't even realize it… or appreciate it, so much."

Laying his hand over the back of hers, his lips began to curl, "That's what husbands are for, right?"

"Yeah," she agreed with a small nod, "That's exactly what husbands are for."

Putting her boots on, the couple made their way downstairs. Deciding to eat a small lunch, Tori stood by the window and stared out into the yard, observing the patches of snow.

Brian entered the room while she waited on her meal, clearing his throat and taking a chair at the table, where her mate sat, watching in silence.

"I hear you're upset with me," he stated calmly, initiating the conversation in French and folding his hands on the wooden surface.

"Well, you know how it is, Danny. You didn't follow directions, but then again, you seldom do."

She didn't move to look at him, which only added to his feelings of resentment. "You decided to use my house and my friends as bait," he puckered his lips, dislike giving way to anger. "You don't see anything wrong with that?"

"No, Danny. Nothing is going to happen to *your* friends. They will be perfectly safe," she raised her shoulders as she spoke, obviously distressed.

Michael clenched his fists as if they were his vocal chords and he were keeping them under control.

"Oh yeah?" Brian countered, "If they're so safe, what difference does it make if we're here?"

"I want Lindsey on a plane; the next one headed for LA," she said stiffly.

"No," he clipped the word sharply.

"What do you mean, *no*," her hair floated as she spun to glare at him.

"She's not leaving," he stated calmly. "She's taking the semester off and staying here… with me."

She stared into the blue eyes that matched her own, waiting for the punch line. When it didn't come, she moved to the table and took a seat. "This is going to be dangerous, Danny."

"You just said my friends weren't in any danger, make up your damn mind. Is it or isn't it?" he sat up straighter in his chair, challenging her to an extent, sharing the glare with her mate.

Stella placed her plate in front of her, and Tori began to pick at her food. "It's different. Not the danger," she could feel the urge to cry sneaking up on her, "The way I feel about it. I don't want anything to happen to you. It petrifies me." He could see the redness of her nose when she looked up.

His mouth opened, his argument hanging in his throat, "Come on sis, we're gonna be fine."

"Will you be fine afterwards? After you've watched what I'm gonna do to those bastards when they get here?" she clenched her jaw, a tear slipping, rolling to drip unchecked.

"Alright, that's enough," Michael intervened, unable to

hold his say any longer. "You and I have talked about this," his hand wafted between his brother-in-law and himself. "I told you about the world she came from, and what she's capable of."

Tori stared at her mate, mouth hanging open, "What I'm capable of?" Her laugh sounded off key, "I'm going to kill them, that's what I'm capable of. I'm going to use my knife, and a gun, and whatever it takes to spill their blood and stop their hearts *forever*." Her teeth were bare as she spoke; her lips drawn back into a snarl, her brow furrowed, "I'm going to destroy them, Danny; are you ready to watch?"

Brian stared at the woman before him, unsure what he should say, or could say for that matter. His jaw clenched, he rapped loudly on the table with a knuckle; his mind turned memories of all that had happened. He recalled all that he had learned since the first time she set foot in his house, and he had spoken down to her in that very room.

"No, baby girl," his mouth moved as if his words took great effort to form, "I'm not gonna watch." He swallowed, his Adam's apple moving up and down, a single tear finding its way over the stubble of his cheek, "I'm gonna help."

He could see the look of horror on her face, and he lurched towards her, stabbing the surface between them, voice rising. "They didn't do this to *just you*!" he screamed, his poked heaving, "All the things that you lost, I lost!" He stabbed himself in the chest with the digit, then pointed it at her, "If you think... that you are the only one that has suffered... the only one in pain... that you're the only one who want's revenge..." his final pause became long, "You're wrong."

Sitting back in his seat, he wiped his face, his hand moving over his mouth. "I'm sorry if that bothers you," his voice returned to normal, and he scooted his chair away from the table, standing and leaving the room.

"What do I do?" she whispered, looking over at her mate with desperation in her eyes.

"We make a plan," he breathed noisily. "And we include him. I have an idea for sparing the others, and we can get Lins out of the way."

"Ok," she nodded, "Then we need to move, put things in order."

"You didn't eat your lunch," he indicated the plate of chicken and vegetables before her. "You need your strength, love." Taking a few bites, she complied while he explained how he intended to get the party guests off the property almost as soon as they arrived.

"Anyone watching the house will be unlikely to know, and we will position ourselves to take out the men once they have arrived," he stated calmly. "I spoke to Brett, and there will be twelve men, the typical formation of a crew. Their leader is named Robert Stroud, but he's the only one he knows by name," he drew on his palm with a finger, as if it were a tally sheet. "So we will be outnumbered, but I think we will have the advantage."

"I like this plan," she half smiled, "I mean, if we don't want to just hide them in the servant's quarters."

"I thought about that," he agreed, "But I'm afraid they would be found."

"Ok," she nodded. "Then we get them out of here."

His nose wrinkled with his laugh, "Ok, let's get to work and be ready." Together, they explained to the others what would take place, and when night fell, they were able to put things in motion.

Well after dark, the cars that carried their guests pulled up out front, and the party fell in full swing; at least it appeared to be. As soon as the two bands and entourage entered, however, it became obvious that everything was not what it seemed.

"We've had a threat," Brian explained, leading the two groups through the hallway, to the kitchen in the back. "And we don't want it to be public, so we're going to sneak you out of here."

From there, Collin would lead the guests and their girls through the darkness of the back yard, into the garage that housed their limo and its driver. "You guys'll have to squeeze in. I know the car wasn't designed for this many people, but it's to get you out of here, so nothing happens to you."

"Is this another publicity stunt?" a male voice spoke up, "Or just an elaborate way of pissing us off?" A wave of agreement swept through the small crowd, followed by a louder rumbling of discontent.

"No, this isn't," Cody tried to clarify. "And what happened in LA wasn't either. We really need to get out of here. All of us!"

"Yeah, right. I came here for a party, man," the guest sauntered over towards the door to the hallway. "And I hear one back the way we came," he left the kitchen, a few of the girls trailing after him.

"Holy shit!" Cody swore loudly, "Do you people not understand what we're saying?"

"Well," Collin spread his arms wide, "We're leaving. We suggest you do the same," he reached for Lindsey's hand to take her with them.

"We can't go and leave them here!" Cody grit his teeth, "Where's Tori?" He began calling her name as the guests began to separate, making themselves at home in the massive structure.

Climbing the back stairs, Cody continued to search for the girl, who had gone down the front stairs at the exact same time. Turning into the front room, she intended to make rounds through the house, not sure when their party crashers would arrive. Instead she found herself face to face with the lead singer from one of the other two bands from the tour.

"What the fuck are you guys doing here?" she called out loudly, in an effort to be heard over the music.

Laughing, another one of them moved to stand in front of her, "I knew this was a hoax. As bad as your hangover during the shoot."

"Hey, I was sick during the photo shoot, and this is serious shit! Danny!" she screamed her brother's name, exiting the room and running into Cody, who was coming down the front stairs.

"There you are," he held his hand out to her, "We have a problem."

"Yeah, no shit," she replied angrily. "What the hell are they still doing here?" she pointed at the living area with a stiff hand, indicating the two bands and their groupies.

"They refused to leave," he said with a shrug. "They think this's a publicity stunt."

"No fucking way," she spun on her heel, making her way over to the stereo system and pulling the plug, causing an abrupt silence. "Listen up!" she bellowed, "This is not a game! This is not a stunt! This is -" she caught her breath, seeing a flash of light through the front glass, "Oh shit!" she finished to herself, breathing heavily.

"Listen to me, do what they say! Do *exactly* what they say!" she commanded, darting for the door and back up the stairs.

"What the hell?" Cody watched her go, hands on his hips.

Before he could move to follow her, the front door came crashing in next to him, the men coming through it waving various sized weapons and shouting, "GET ON YOUR KNEES! GET ON YOUR KNEES!" The Spiders, brandishing their weapons, grabbed anyone who refused to

150

listen and forced them to comply, pushing them to kneel and zip tying their hands behind their backs.

One of the guests laughed, "Hey this is pretty good! I may have to do this at my next party." A moment later, he lay on the floor, blood pouring out of his mouth and nose.

"Shoot him?" his assailant called loudly, holding a pistol to the back of his head.

"Negative," came the voice of Robert Stroud, in an authoritative reply. "First we find the girl. Check these bitches; you know she's gotta be here somewhere."

Handling the women roughly, they continued to search, talking to one another on their handheld devices as they spread out to go through the remainder of the house. Fifteen minutes later, they had rounded up everyone they could locate in the structure, and had them gathered on the floor in the front room, including the servants and head of security.

"Where the fuck is she?" Robert called out loudly, "Somebody answer me!" Recognizing Cody, he pulled out a 9 mm pistol and held it to his head, "Where's the girl?"

"I-I-I don't know what girl," he lied flatly, while on his knees and struggling to hold his balance with his bound appendages, causing the women in the room to squeal and cry loudly at his movements.

"Don't fuck with me, I'll shoot you right here! I know you're in a band with her – where is she?"

"Upstairs," he stammered, "She ran upstairs."

"Carl," Robert called into his hand held, "Go sweep upstairs. That's where she went."

Labyrinth of Lies

Tori clung to the trellis, her heart pounding in her ears. She had climbed out the window before, only a few weeks ago, and didn't relish the idea of doing it again. However, since their house had been overrun by hoodlums, as her old friend Marge would have called them, she didn't really have a choice.

Leaning into the dried shrubs, she wished there were green leaves on them so that she would have more cover. Surveying the ground below her, she focused on her breathing and could see only one man left outside. The rest were presumably inside turning the place upside down and looking for her. *I'm glad I pulled the plug on the music;* she praised herself wryly. *At least now I'll be able to hear the shots when they start killing my friends.*

Looking up, she could see the window that she had closed behind her, wondering if they would think to check outside of it. Deciding she needed to move, she began to make her way down as quietly as she could, until her feet were on the ground. *I better check the back;* she ticked off her checklist. *I'm certain they have it covered.*

Sure enough, she could see the glossy leather glinting under the light of the moon, the man posted at the kitchen entrance pacing back and forth. Pausing, his back turned to her when he moved to light a cigarette, she silently made her way towards him, until the pop of her blade before it cut his throat. Gripping him firmly, she dragged him away from the area, dropping his body in the shadows on the side of the house.

Quietly, she made her way around to the front, approaching from the side of the opposite living area, keeping low. Pushing herself up, she peered in and could view the empty room, with movement across the foyer. *Good, they haven't moved them.*

Seeing that the front door had been kicked in, she studied the man standing with his back to it for a moment. *Can't attack him there; I would be seen.* Sliding back, she moved away from the house, taking a position next to a large tree and began tapping on the bark with the butt of her knife. TAP-TAP-TAP, followed by silence. TAP-TAP-TAP, again followed by silence.

Breathing deeply, she kept her heart rate under control, noticing her target had heard the sound, and had begun moving through the shrubs to investigate. Remaining in the shadow of the tree, she waited patiently until he came into position, then she leapt out at him, catching him in the head and knocking him to the ground. Their struggle brief, it ended with a loud pop before her weapon of choice found the line of his jaw, where it met his neck.

Wiping the blood from the blade onto his shirt, the girl turned, moving back to the house and climbing the trellis to her room. The light from the hallway gave the space an eerie glow, and she could see that it remained unoccupied. Forcing the window to slide, she wiggled back inside; moving over next to her bed, she lay still and listened. She could hear loud voices from outside, and presumed that they continued to search for her.

Standing, she glided over to the door, noting the crackle of a voice giving commands, becoming aware they were using a radio of some kind. Hovering in the doorframe, she waited, listening to the footsteps on the carpet go into the room across from hers; *one man,* she breathed to herself, *easy money.*

Leaving her room, she stood next to the wall. Waiting for him to exit, she slowly pulled her pistol. The man stepped past her, eager to move to the room she had just exited. She caught him with the bottom of the handle, knocking him to the floor, shoving her knee in his back and holding the gun at the base of his skull, "Don't move!" she hissed.

Listening for a moment, she could still hear the commotion downstairs, and the voice called out over his handheld again, "Carl... Carl!"

The man shifted slightly beneath her, and she dug the tip of her weapon in deeper. "I said don't move!" at the same time putting the nine in her left hand and retrieving her knife with the right.

When he heard the catch spring on the blade, he rolled to knock her off of himself, but too late to prevent the motion. She took out the third with a small grin, cleaning the blade once more and catching his foot to drag him the rest of the way into the bedroom, leaving his body hidden by the bed.

Back in the hall, she traveled to the far end, where she caught her fourth man coming up the stairs, she presumed to investigate what happened to Carl. In the end, it didn't matter; she left his body on the landing and continued down the stairs and into the kitchen. Peeking into the wide room, she wasn't able to see anyone, and knew that it would be a long journey to the front of the house.

Darting silently, she made her way around the corner, pausing in the hallway for a moment, pressed against the wall, when she heard the distinct sound of her husband, calling her name. It sounded faint, and definitely coming from the front of the house.

Her steps slow and silent, she hugged the wall; pistol in

her hands, she continued towards the living area. The voices were becoming clearer as she got closer.

"Call her again!" a male voice commanded, followed by silence; she could hear him being struck before he cried her name.

"Tori!" her mate's voice rang out, followed by semi quiet. The sound of shrieks from some of the women in the room, muffled and faint, filtered down the hall.

"This's bullshit, man! I'm telling you; she ran off. She left these guys here, and took the fuck off!" the speaker had been unfamiliar.

"Carl!" the voice called again, and she could tell he was keying a mic. "Stan!" the man waited about ten seconds, then repeated, "Stan!"

Tori had reached the edge of the doorway and remained pressed against the wall. On the far wall above the staircase hung a portrait of the band. Using the reflection on the glass, she could see into the room, or at least partially into the room. Her husband knelt on the floor, his hands behind his back, center or close to the door. Next to him stood a Spider, who angrily spoke into his phone.

"Stan!" he called again, and Tori could see his boots, next to the threshold, realizing he stood almost near enough to touch.

Swift, controlled movement, she swung into the room, placing the tip of her nine inches from the speaker's head, "That's enough!"

Inhaling deeply, the man raised his hands slowly.

"Was Stan the skinny bastard in the back? Or the fat fuck in the front?" she taunted him.

The leader stood frozen, holding his hands up in front of his chest, still gripping the device, "Well, well, well… if it ain't Tori Farrell. Been lookin' forward to this."

"I bet you have," she replied in a deeper voice than

normal, keeping her gaze fixed on her target while flicking her eyes quickly to assessed the remainder of the room. "You're running low on men, you know that?" she teased.

"Am I?" he shot back, looking over at his second, "You're still outnumbered, bitch."

"Yup," she agreed, meeting Michael's gaze for a brief moment, noticing that Cody knelt on the floor next to him, about a yard away. "Hey listen, Robert," she called softly, "It is Robert, isn't it?" Mason and Eli were among the captured, *why aren't they dead? What the fuck are these guys up to?*

"Yeah," he grinned, turning slightly, "In fact it is."

"I thought so," she smiled as well. "Robert, I think we need to make a deal, you and I."

"I'm listening," his voice remained calm.

"I won't kill any more of your men," she continued to glance around, aware that Enrique and Brett were the only two not among the captives, "And I'll even go with you, if you'll leave these people alone." For emphasis, she nodded towards the musicians and their girls. "Leave them here, alive and unharmed, and I'll go with you, wherever you wanna go. My life… for theirs."

"Oh, you know that's against the rules," he breathed in an airy fashion.

"Yeah, but who's gonna care?" she turned on the charm. "All the reps are gone, babe. It's just you an' me, now," her voice grew quieter. "Let these guys go, an' let's get outta here."

"And then what?" he demanded quietly.

"Whatever you like," she tilted her head, smiling. "I used to be quite talented, you know. I was Eddie's prize. I mean, we've never met, but maybe you've heard of me."

"Oh, I've heard o' you all right. A murderin' whore, tha's what you are," he sneered, turning to point a finger at her brother. "Does he know? Has he heard what you're good for?" his laughter low, he pushed at her to make a move; she didn't budge.

"Yeah, he knows."

"And I guess that means they all know, huh," he waved a hand slightly at the rest of their hostages. "Filthy cunt," he cursed her, "I don't think I'm taking your little bargain. I'm gonna kill you, an' I'm gonna kill all your little friends. And I'm even gonna let 'em watch all of us fuck you before we do."

Tori's gaze fixed on the man, her peripheral caught the movement of reflected light through the front glass.

"Is that so," she fidgeted with her gun, moving her feet slightly to work her way into the room. Her left arm remained stiff; pistol pointed at his face. The Spiders were spread about the area; the remaining eight all accounted for. "You know," she changed tactics, "I really hope you have your affairs in order."

He began to laugh, "Why, you think you stand a chance? Or are you gonna pull the ol' 'I may not get you all, but I'm gonna get you' routine."

"Nope," she replied crisply, then nodded slightly, "I'm gonna get you all," she breathed with confidence. She shifted a few more inches, close enough to Michael she could reach him if she wanted. Able to see down his back, his hands did not appear to be bound. Her eyes back on Robert, he glared at her, and she could make out Brett moving in the reflection of the glass in the foyer.

"I don't think you are," their attacker whispered loudly, swinging into action, shooting his hand up towards her weapon.

Anticipating his move, she lifted the gun, pivoting around the room and firing three shots, catching three of the Spiders cleanly before dropping it into her husband's hands. Continuing her spin, she caught the group's leader in the jaw with a leaping kick and they both fell to the floor.

At the sound of the shots, Enrique and Brett charged into the room, taking out the remainder of the Spiders with Michael getting one of his own while Tori flicked her blade open in mid-swing, plunging it into the leaders belly and cutting him across the middle.

Sinking to the floor, his innards spilling into his hands, he gasped loudly, choking in agony. Kicking him in the face, she stood, watching while he rolled over, clawing at the floor as if he could crawl away. Her hand covered in blood; Tori looked down at her trembling digits, turning to take in the rest of the crowded room, and calling loudly, "Anyone hurt?"

Brett had begun moving through and cut everyone free.

Not getting any responses, Tori grasped at her husband, running her fingers over his face where he'd been beaten, "How are you, love?"

"I'm fine," he pulled her against him, pressing his forehead against the side of her head. Looking over at her brother, she twisted free, moving to inspect him.

"Danny?" her voice barely audible, her hands bloodied his shirt as she anxiously stroked him, shaking as they raked over his chest and torso.

"I'm good," he replied, turning himself to check on Lindsey, who threw her arms around his waist, clinging to him and sobbing.

Casting a quick gaze around the group, her eyes lit upon Eli, who calmly walked towards the door, phone in hand. *Checking in with Godfry, more than likely.* "Sit still guys," she commanded, "The police will be here any minute." Finding her mate, she sufficed herself to grip him, and wait for the Feds.

Enrique moved up behind her to create a Tori sandwich between them, "Good work, baby girl," he cooed into her hair, his hands on her hips.

"You two aren't fighting over me again, are you?" she teased.

"No," Enrique whispered so that only the three of them could hear, his hand sliding around to her belly, "But I don't cares if you're carryin' his kid, you're old man's gonna have to share."

Let it Ring

Tori could feel the eyes of everyone in the room upon them. *Of course, I killed half a dozen men in front of them so that could be why they're staring.* Laying her blood stained fingers over Enrique's, she matched his tone, keeping her words private as well, "We don't know that I'm pregnant, baby. Only a theory at this point."

"He's still gonna share," he breathed across her ear. "I've come too far to give up on you."

Lifting her chin, her eyes locked on the brown orbs of her mate, her stomach did a somersault when he used a whisper as well, "You treat her with respect, Enrique. That's all that I ask."

The man behind her tightened his grip for a moment, then released her, "You love her your way, and I'll love her mine. My kinda respect."

Moving so she could see them both, she smiled, "Please don't fight over me, guys. I don't think I could ever really choose between you." Pulling herself away, she headed towards the door, hoping to find out when the Feds would arrive.

To her surprise, there were cars already in the driveway, and James Godfry climbed out of one of them. "Holy shit," she muttered, taking a few wide strides to get to him, "What the hell are you doing here?" Seeing Eli on the steps, she quickly deduced that he had told his boss their plan before it had been carried out.

"Don't be angry," Jim interrupted her thoughts, "He did it for you."

"Did what for me?" she cut her eyes over at him, "Put our plan in jeopardy by sharing it with you?"

"I'm not the enemy, Tori. I'll admit, I've made some poor choices; but I always did what I thought was right."

"Wow, that sounds awfully familiar. Did you and Eli practice that line together?" she fumed.

Drawing a deep breath, he refused to be drawn into a debate with her. "Let's move inside." At the front of the room, he made an announcement, "I need everyone who took part in the violence to come with me. The rest of you will be interviewed separately." Enrique, Brett and Michael all stepped forward, her husband reaching and catching her hand to entwine their fingers.

"Follow me please," Jim turned and led them down the hall, stopping in the kitchen, "Well, this will do. If you want to wash yourself in the sink, you may do so," he offered, his eyes dropping to the girl's hands. "I'm sure that blood isn't comfortable."

"No, it isn't," she quickly agreed, moving to give them a scrubbing.

"Have a seat, fellas," he addressed the men, indicating the large square table. "I wanted to commend you all on a job well done," he began when she had joined them.

"What makes you think we did a good job?" Brett demanded. "Those men're dead. Lawmen typically frown on that sort o' thing."

"Yes, they do," Jim agreed. "But I have been after those men, as well as the ones that employed them, for the better part of a decade." His gaze shifted over to the girl, "You've done a right fine job, Tori. You should be proud of yourself."

"Forgive me if I don't agree," she countered softly.

"And that is what makes you special," the agent grinned. "I'm going to reinstate Mason and Eli. They will be heading up the task force that will be attacking the Ramirez brothers in a few days."

Tori stared at him, her jaw dropping wide. "*We* are going after them, like you wanted us to," she tossed out loudly. "You can't take this away from us. Let us finish this!"

"I'm afraid I can't do that, not in your condition," he stated flatly.

"My condition?" her voice grew shrill. Her eyes darting between Enrique and her husband, "Everyone is assuming they know what's going on, but we don't know that for sure. I haven't been tested or been to the doctor. This could be something else entirely!"

"Eli told me you'd be upset," Jim tried to console her. "And I want you to know, he isn't doing this to hurt you. He's doing it because he cares."

"Bullshit," she spat angrily, "Let us finish this shit, so we know that we are safe. So we know that it's done. So we can get on with our lives and put this behind us." Her heart stopped, aware they could be arrested for their actions, "Or are you sending us to prison?"

"Prison? No," he shook his head. "You will all be given clemency for your contribution to this case. Go back to Texas. All of you. Get some rest, and we'll let you know when it's over."

Standing, the agent's chubby legs made for the door, leaving the four of them seated at the table. Enrique stared at Michael, wondering if the other man had meant what he said, and if he would get a turn with her at last. Shifting to the girl, he folded his hands on the table before him, "It's getting late. I think we needs to get some sleep, and decides what we're gonna do in the morning."

"Agreed," Michael could see him staring at her.

Reaching over, he squeezed her arm, "Brett and I'll take care of whatever needs to be handled with the Feds and the bodies. You go get some rest."

Brett's eyes popped open with surprise, but he stood along with sandy-haired man, following him out into the hall. Unable to resist, he demanded quietly, "You're jus' gonna hand her over to 'im?"

"No," Michael paused, leaning on the wall so they could talk. "I've known for a while that they have... feelings... for each other. I wouldn't dare ask her to choose between us. I'm not sure that I would win that kind of fight, even if she chose me." He looked over at the older man, hoping he understood.

"Wow," Brett laughed. "So you're jus' gonna share. That's awesome! When do I get my turn?" The taller man spun around, laying his arm across his chest and shoving him against the wall.

"This isn't a game, Brett. If you don't like how things are, look the other way! And keep your mouth shut while you're at it," he released him, glaring into his green eyes. "If she were to choose you, that would be up to her. I'm trying to keep an open mind, and hold on to what I have – end of story."

Turning his back, Michael moved down the hall, eager to end the awkward conversation and do something productive.

Brett ran his fingers tensely around his lips, glancing back at the kitchen door, and then slowly followed behind.

Seated in the kitchen, Enrique had watched them leave, an odd feeling in the pit of his stomach. "Is he toying with us?"

"No," she leaned on her hand, staring at him across the wide table. "He told me on New Year's Eve that he didn't care if we were together."

Enrique sneered, "Really. And you didn't come running straight to me?"

She laughed, her head making it all the way to the flat surface, "I've been trying really hard to do what's right."

"You means to conform," he stood up, moving around to pull on her chair. "Come on, baby girl; you're exhausted."

Rising, she complied with his request, in no condition to argue, "What's wrong with being like everyone else? What's so bad about wanting a normal life?"

"Nothing, I guess," he slid his arm around her, guiding her to the stairs, "Only, who decides what's normal?" She climbed the steps beside him, not bothering to respond. When they reached the top, he stopped her, "You're not gonna argue with me about that?"

"I know where you're going with it," she sighed, "And there isn't any argument for it. People have been debating about who gets the say since time began. For every *Anti*-there's a *Pro*-. Neither side is *right*."

"Exactly," he leaned forward, closing his eyes and brushing his lips against hers.

Tori's breath caught in her lungs, her hands on his chest, holding him where he stood. Nuzzling him with her nose, she could feel the thrill of the moment before she became aware that they were not alone on the floor. At the far end of the hall, they were removing the body from her and Michael's bedroom.

"Let's gos to mine," Enrique suggested, turning her by her elbow and guiding her down the hall. "I don't wanna sleep in his bed anyways."

"Oh, you think we're going to spend the night together?" she peeked at him with a small grin, which he ignored for the time being.

Inside the room, he closed the door behind them, his heart pounded. Moving up behind her, his body matched hers, standing only close enough to tease. "I don't think we should get too dirty," he kept his tone low, "I don't want to hurt you, or anything," his voice trailed away, refusing to mention her 'condition' again, or imply that she was fragile.

"You've changed a lot, Enrique," she turned, maintaining their closeness. "You're not the same man who pinned me to the wall in the halfway house," she giggled at the memory, "And scared the shit out of me when he did."

His fingers toying with a curl of ebony hair, he agreed, "No, I'm really not. That man was self-absorbed. He didn't love you. He never loved or cared about anyone, maybe not even himself."

"You said that you did," she challenged.

"Wells, yeah, I did. I said it to lots of girls, 'cause those words are like magic." He grinned, his pride getting the better of him for a moment. "I wanted to get to you, baby girl; to get you to gos with me so's I could give you to Brett and get my place back. I didn't care about you, or what would happen to you when I did."

She stared at him, her heart heavy, "It was a lie."

"Yeah, it was a lie," he ran his hand around her waist, massaging her back, "Right up to the last night we were together before I skipped out. That was when I realized the person I had been lying to, was myself. I did love you, and I've been trying to convince you of that ever since."

"Well, just so you know, it wasn't those words that convinced me," she leaned her forehead against his, her breathing slowing to almost nothing. "I liked that you said there was an *us*, and I have never forgotten that feeling. The way that you made me feel special. But in the end, that's not what made me believe."

His face brushed against hers, his fingers toying with her hair behind her back, "What convinced you, baby girl? How did you sees the truth?"

She nuzzled his stubble coated jaw, "You gave me away."

His body went stiff, completely taken by surprise, "What's that?"

Her hands made their way to his chest; she unbuttoned his over shirt, her fingers finding the cotton below, "You told me you were there. You said you thought we were a couple, but I don't believe that." She squinted at him, "You left me with him because it was better for me. You wanted me to have a better life. A normal one."

He clasped her hands inside of his, "That's not why I did it," he denied.

"Ok, then why did you?"

His brown orbs drilled into to her, and she waited for his response. Finally, he caved, "Is it always gonna be like this?"

"Like what?" she cajoled.

"I've never had a girl I couldn't lies to," he licked his lips, "Who could sees through me and knew the truth that was in my heart. How do you do that?"

She smiled hard, causing her eyes to squint, "I told you, remember? I get vibes from people. They tell me what I need to know."

"I knew it," he breathed, leaning his face next to hers, "You are a witch." He lips suctioned lightly against hers, moving, searching and tasting.

She parted hers, deepening the kiss, putting her hands back on his chest and pushing his shirt away, allowing it to fall to the floor.

Sliding her fingers up to his shoulders, she fondled the seams of the tank undershirt that he wore, recalling the day that she had helped him pick out the clothes, and tracing the line of his muscles. "You do something to me," she whispered, keeping her face close to his, "I love Michael, Enrique; I need you to know that." She flicked her eyes open to stare into his, "But there's a part of me that doesn't belong to him. It belongs to you."

Pushing her mouth forward, she kissed him forcefully, her fingers pulling at the rest of his clothing to undress him. Sliding out of her jeans and tee, she trembled at the feel of his hands on her flesh, his digits unclasping her bra and sliding it down her arms, dropping it on the floor.

Her nipples were drawn up tight when he touched them, not as pink as he thought they had been. Pushing her towards the bed, he breathed, "We need a word, a safe word they call it. Something you can use to let me know when I've gone too far, and I need to stop."

"I don't need a safe word, Enrique," she smiled, biting at his neck, thrilled by the sweet salt of his flesh. "I trust you, baby. Do what you want with me, and leave me breathless."

Her words were like fire, scorching his mind and soul. Pulling at her panties, he couldn't wait any longer, "I'm gonna hurt you, baby girl. I'm gonna pull your hair and slap your ass, and make you beg me to do it again."

Her moan loud when he pushed himself inside her, the folds of flesh had become drenched from their foreplay. "Do it baby, as hard as you like."

He lifted her leg, "Oh, trusts me, it's mine, and I'm gonna make sure you know it." He thrust against her, the pain exhilarating, causing her to cry out in small chirps that only encouraged him. After a few minutes, he pushed himself in, holding still until he could move again.

Withdrawing from her, he flipped her onto her belly, pulling her up onto her knees so that he could stand behind her. Pushing himself back into her roughly, the round pucker above her folds teased him, and he slid his thumb across it, causing it to squirm.

"Man, if I had some gel…"

"I thought we weren't going nasty," she called to him between pants, aware that she really wanted to feel him inside her.

Gathering her juices onto his thumb, he pushed it through the folds of skin, "My GOD, baby girl, you're killing me." Gathering more, he switched to his longer digits, "I'll use my fingers untils we can get some."

She pushed back hard against him, her mind lost in the desire to be stretched and filled, his body slapping against her mercilessly. Grasping at her breasts, she stopped their bouncing, aware that it was uncomfortable, but not enough to ask him to stop.

Reaching out, he grabbed her hair, pulling on it in a large wad. Her fingers squeezing the bedding, she began to cry out loudly, her voice sharp. His fingers found her mound of flesh and pressed it hard against her pubic bone, sending her over the edge, trembling and screaming as he finished himself inside her.

Pushing her forward, onto the bed, he sprawled across the top of her, and she breathed, "That wasn't making love, was it?" panting heavily against the bed.

"Making love? Hells no," his words were separated by the need for air, "That was good ol' fashioned fucking, why?"

"Because, that's what Michael told me," she fought to push herself up slightly, "He didn't want me to make love to you."

Enrique burst into laughter, sliding over to the side and allowing her to get up, "No worries baby girl; remember we tried that once. Wasn't so great. We sticks to what we're good at." He got up, pushing her over onto her back and spreading her legs, his juices oozed out of her, and he grabbed himself, waiting for his need to be renewed.

Staring up at him, she placed her palm along his jaw, her breathing slowing, "I think I've had enough, baby." She smiled, sad that she couldn't go longer.

Catching her hand, he brought it around and pressed the

fleshy pads to his lips, inhaling the scent of her, "No worries, baby girl. I'll take what I can gets."

Laying over her, he smoothed her hair, entwining his fingers with hers. "I'm jealous ya know," he kissed and nuzzled her lips and face. "You wear his ring and took his name."

"Yeah, well, you get me a ring, and I'll wear yours, too," she teased. "The name, I'm sorry, but I can't really help that."

"You're gonna wear two rings on your finger?"

"No silly," she giggled, "I have other fingers. It's what's in your heart that counts. A ring without love... is just a ring."

He nodded, staring down at her and wondering how she could always make things so clear. "I love you, Tori," he sighed, kissing her forehead. "And I'll do that; I'll find one that's special to me, to give to you."

"Oh, baby," she replied softly, pushing him up so that she could slide between the sheets. Spooning up behind her, he allowed her to face the window, sprawling slightly across the center of the bed. Looping her fingers with his, his heart flopped heavily when he heard the unmistakable sound of her sweet voice whisper into the darkness, "Yes baby, I love you, too."

You Don't Say

The following morning, the members of the household were unusually quiet when they gathered in the kitchen. Stella prepared a large breakfast, and everyone fixed their plates, sitting around the table to eat and discuss their course of action.

"I guess the band is back together," Brian tossed out, smiling at the petite blonde who took her seat next to him.

"Yeah," Tori agreed quietly, her mind still trapped in the darkness and the greedy sex she had shared with Enrique. Neither of them had mentioned their encounter to Michael, and he would never ask, as there are some things you don't say. Reaching over, her mate caressed her back, and she sat up straighter in her chair, giving him a small smile, grateful for his understanding.

"I still need to be gone for a few days," she reminded the group. "After that, we'll know if I will be able to do it. I hate to make any real commitments until we know more."

"Are you still sick?" Brian's face grew dark. "Last night, you looked pretty healthy when you were taking care of those guys."

"No, Danny; I was never really sick," she admitted in a quiet tone, aware that only the men who were with her on their quest knew of her condition.

"So what's going on, then," he demanded.

"She's pregnant," Enrique blurted, overcome with a

surge of joy at the awareness of it, even if the baby wasn't biologically his.

An awkward silence followed, the gathering staring at the three of them. Tori and Michael gave him a concerned look.

"Sorry," he apologized. "That really wasn't my news to shares, was it," he flushed slightly, stirring his eggs nervously.

"How can you be pregnant?" Lindsey asked in shock, "I thought you couldn't have babies."

Tori smiled at her friend, wishing she wasn't still upset that she had been there. "I've been seeing a doctor, who was trying to help me heal so that we could try. And it looks like he was successful," she grinned shyly, flicking her gaze at Enrique, "And it's ok, baby; I know you're happy, too."

He nodded in an exaggerated manner, "Very happy for you, baby girl."

"So we may not play together after all," Collin spoke up, running his fingers through his hair. "I have to say; things around here were a hell of a lot calmer before you came along."

"Yeah, I bet so. Anyways, Michael and I are going back to Texas this afternoon, and will stay there until after my appointment, and we'll let you know what we find out," she informed them non-committal.

"You know we're going with you," Enrique spoke up, no longer afraid of making his feelings known. "I mean, that's what I thought we would do."

"Actually," Brett interceded, "Since we've officially been relieved o' duty by th' FBI, I was thinkin' o' remainin' here. You know, t' stay on as security for th' band, since your other guy quit last night an' all."

His comment sent the group into fits of laughter at the tantrum Pete had thrown before storming out of the house. "We won't miss him much," Cody declared. "And I think you would be great, if anyone wants my opinion."

"Yeah," Brian agreed, "You sure you don't want to stay, too?" he shifted his gaze over at Enrique. "Give these two some time alone together?" he indicated his sibling and brother-in-law with his fork as he spoke.

Tori shifted in her seat, aware that the man to her right had grown tense, obviously trying to decide how to protect her from being outed about their relationship. To her surprise, her husband spoke up.

"Enrique's going with us. We're going to put him to work in the shop, aren't we, love?" he winked at his wife, giving her a half grin.

"Sure," she replied softly. "Always things to do around there," she returned his smile.

"Uh-huh," Brian grunted, almost letting it go. "You know, you three… are weird. I just want you to know that."

Angry, Tori pushed herself back, ready to go upstairs and prepare to leave, "Why are we weird, Danny? Because it's a girl and two guys? I guess it'd be ok if Michael and I had decided we wanted to bring another girl in with us." Her eyes flicked to her young friend, aware that she may have been clueless as to what was going on.

Michael and Enrique shot each other a look, and then both began to protest, but she cut them off. "Stop, ok? I know what you guys are going to say, and that's not the point. The point is; it's *our choice*. Who cares if we are or if we're not, because in the end, it's our business, and the rest of you fuckers can just stay out of it." She had made it to it to the stairs, headed up and not bothering to look back.

Tori sorted through her clothes, deciding what she might like to take home with her when her husband joined her. "I'm sorry," she blurted as soon as he stood beside her. "I know that we embarrassed you."

"You didn't embarrass me," he defended easily, "In fact,

I'm quite proud of you, and the way you stood up to them. You're right; it's no one's business. I guess you enjoyed yourself last night?"

Her face shot up to stare at him, *son of a bitch. I guess he's going to ask after all.* "I'm sorry; I didn't think you would want to know about it," she stammered.

"It's ok," he shrugged. "I can tell you're more relaxed. I'm glad."

"You know, it doesn't mean that I don't love you," she tossed out eagerly, terrified there might be a price for it in the end.

"I know, baby girl," he laughed loudly. "I know you love me. And, I know you love him, too. I would almost say you have feelings for Brett, but I think he's a little old for you."

She stared at him, rolling her tongue for a moment. "How do you know that?" she finally demanded. "I never said, so what makes you think that."

"I don't know," he shrugged. "You didn't kill him when you took out the Scorpions. I've seen the way he looks at you and touches you sometimes, and you respond to him. Genuine things, not like when you're, I hate to say manipulating; but yeah, when you're not doing that."

"You think that I manipulate people?" she stared at him, the air pressing tightly against the walls of her chest.

"Come on, love, don't do this. I don't want to have a fight with you."

"Then tell me why you said that; that I manipulate people."

"Because you do," he kept a straight face. "You're damn good at it. You are one of those liars that can put the truth in one hand and a straight up lie in the other, and no one can tell them apart. Sometimes, not even you."

"Well, I'm glad I finally get to know what you really think of me!" she sputtered.

"Hey, stop that!" he commanded, "What I think of you? I think you're an incredible person. You're damn smart, beautiful; and fun to be around. I love you, and I can't imagine my life without you. Those things are as much a part of you as the parts you're all pissed off about, and I love them all. You are a combination of so many things, like darkness and light. I may only be able to fulfill part of that, but I would never ask you to give up the rest of who you are for me. I love you, either way."

She stared at him, not sure that she believed him, or why he would love her if that's how he truly perceived her. "So, how does this thing with Enrique work," she tossed her arms across her chest. "Since we're being honest and putting it all out there. Are we going to give him a room at the house and everything?"

"If that's what you want," he shrugged, "I have no problem with that. I really am ok with it. I wasn't sure that I would be, but last night, when I was alone, I had some time to think about things. When you get to the bottom line, I love every crazy thing about you. Your lies, your past, your... everything. And we're going to have a baby! Doesn't that give you a little bit of excitement?"

Tori looked away, a wide grin crossing her face, "Yes it does, but I'm trying to *not* get too excited, until we see what the doctor says. A lot of things can still go wrong."

"I know," he agreed, his grin broad, his voice chipper, "But its ok. We'll face it together. All three of us. So let's get packed and get out of here." Reaching over, he slid his arm around her waist, and she kissed him lightly, secretly elated to be going home.

Stranger Things

Leaving his wife to tend to her packing, Michael made his way down to the opposite end of the hall. Finding Enrique's door open, he walked inside, "How's it goin'?"

The other man cast a wary glance, "Hey Mike. It's going. Have to admit, I's a little surprised you wants me to go with the two of yous to Texas. Figured you'd be ready to get rid of me by now."

"Naw, hard to admit, but you and I are a lot alike. More than either of us knew, until we were out on the road together." He shoved his hands in his pockets, "Besides, she needs us both."

Enrique pursed his lips, not sure how to respond to such a statement, or that he could agree.

"Anyways, I wanted you to know that we're going to give you a bedroom at the house. And you'll be welcome there for as long as you like," Michael finished smoothly.

Enrique stopped moving, his arm hanging over the pack he had been filling, "What's the catch?"

"There's no catch. I think we understand each other pretty well. And we both want the same thing," Michael smiled as he spoke. "We both love her, and that's what matters."

"And you think we're gonna all three lives together, all happy an' shit," the other man stared at him, still frozen.

"Yeah," he nodded. "Don't ever hurt her, and don't break

her heart. And some day, I think you and I may actually be friends." With that, he turned his back, making his way to the door.

"And what makes you think that?" Enrique yelled after him.

"I dunno," Michael called from around the corner, "Stranger things have happened."

Taking the private plane that afternoon, the trio flew to Denver to retrieve their new bikes. The weather still cold, they would ease their way south, and that made all three of them happy. Tori had been nervous since leaving New York, watching the two men with reserved curiosity and unable to hide her joy at their new arrangement.

Picking out a motel for the night, the three of them stood out front, the moment of truth at hand; one room or two. "Which is it going to be?" Michael prodded, prepared to go with majority rule.

"I says one," Enrique positioned himself behind her, arms snaking around her midsection while he grinned at the other man.

Michael swallowed with a straight face, aware that he had no real desire to watch him with her, but not wanting to let on that he felt squeamish about it either. "Tori?" He could see the look of panic cross her features.

"I'm good with whatever you choose," she dumped it back in his lap.

He eyed the two of them, chewing his lower lip for a moment. *We are going to share a house, after all,* he told himself firmly. "Alright, I'll be right back." He left the pair standing together while he went inside to get the key.

"Are you nervous?" Enrique breathed in her ear, still holding her from behind.

"A little bit. He's never really been on the road; not like we have," she explained. "Or at least, he didn't enjoy it. I'm nervous for him."

His hand slid up to fondle her breast gently, "Don't worry. I'll go easy on him. Maybe even hold off on the fucking for the night, and just… settles in."

Tori spun in his grasp, facing him, "Not a bad idea." She touched her lips to his, holding him and caressing his neck and hair, then smiling at her mate when he returned. "So, what'd we get?" she called playfully.

"One," he replied, waving the key card at her before sliding it into his pocket, "It's this way." He started his bike and led them around the building to their room.

Inside their quarters, they dropped their packs on the single king sized bed. Tori's heart in her throat, her mouth hung open, *oh shit,* the fear in her chest her own.

Michael sidled up to her, watching Enrique poke around, "Close your mouth, love."

Tori obeyed, clamping it shut and reaching for him.

His arm around her waist, he kissed her, "I love you."

"Yeah," she breathed in short pants, "I'm scared."

"Scared of what?" his fingers toyed with hers.

"I want things to be ok."

"Things are ok," he reassured her, "Relax. Get ready for bed."

"Ok," she nodded, removing her jeans and bra and sliding into the covers, taking the center. Lying on her back, she stared at the ceiling and breathed with puffed cheeks, her arms lying above the blankets, on top of her body.

Enrique watched her for a moment, then pulled off his own clothing down to his briefs and climbed onto the bed on her right, laying half above the covers and holding himself up on his elbow. "You knows," he watched the other man do the same, "I've never actually seen this house of yours."

"It's nice," Tori supplied, flicking her eyes over at him. "Lots of room."

Michael lifted the bedspread and climbed under, pushing his body up against hers and laying his arm across her. "Plenty of room," he chimed in. "Needs a lot of work, though. We were in the process of restoring it when her brother had the wreck and everything that has happened since." He laid his head next to hers, "Breathe, baby girl. We're not going to hurt you."

Tori could feel his fingers as he toyed with her hand, fidgeting with her ring. His face rested against her ear, spewing warm air against her scalp. Cutting her eyes over, Enrique's brown orbs were studying her. "We didn't turn out the light," she pointed out, her voice small.

"No," her husband whispered into her hair. "Do you want it off?"

"Are we going to sleep?" she queried, unsure how she felt about it.

"I got some gel," Enrique offered. "In case you wanna lets me use it," his finger grazed the cheek on his side.

Michael shifted, and she could feel his hardness pressing against her thigh. "I've never been between two men because I wanted to be," her chest heaved. "Red and Eddied used to tie me… hang me from the roof, and…"

"I know," Enrique's voice soothed, his fingers catching a whiff of hair, "I saw. In Florida, the first time I tasted you. But, we're not them, baby girl. I think we need that safe word… even if you never use it."

"No," she shifted, "I'm safe. I know I'm safe," she curled her fingers with Enrique's. "But I think I need you guys to take the lead. I'm so petrified; I'm doing good to work my lungs."

Using a free hand, Michael seized the covers, pulling them down to reveal her shirt. Grabbing it, he pushed it up to expose her breasts, and used a delicate touch to outline her nipples, and caress her rose. "Promise me you're not going to hurt her," he lifted his eyes to meet Enrique's. "I've never used gel on anyone before. It looks like it hurts."

"Of course it hurts," Enrique countered. "That's why she likes it."

Tori flicked her eyes between them, her bare skin catching fire. Releasing her lover's hand, she bolted up, pushing Michael over onto his back and snatching the cotton tee to lift it over her head.

Removing her panties eagerly, she straddled his legs and yanked at his briefs, working them down so that his hardened manhood stood up before her. Grasping the shaft, she took the head of him into her mouth, toying with him and tracing the edges with her tongue before sliding him down her throat.

Emitting a quiet moan, she became lost in her desire, pouring herself over her mate. Her fingers gliding across his hips and groin, she became eager to please him.

While she toiled, she could feel Enrique behind her, his fingers gently exploring her, then becoming rougher as he applied the gel. Swaying as the digits worked her, large clumps of her mane fell forward, covering her husband's chest in a thick carpet of ebony locks.

Michael's hand caught the dark waves that had fallen over her face, pushing them aside, as they obstructed his view. Holding the shimmering curtain out of the way, he smiled at what lay before him; her mouth caressing and cajoling his tender flesh, and aware that the other man manipulated hers.

The girl remained focused on the task before her, working to please him. She could feel her pulse in her throat, her heart racing at the excitement their actions produced. A deep ache formed in the pit of her soft folds, her body growing eager to be filled and stretched. Her hollow made sticky crackles as Enrique fingered her, pushing her along and preparing her, first with one finger, then with two.

A moment later, the man behind grabbed her hips, pulling himself up and slipping inside her warm folds easily, fucking her with full hard strokes. Reaching forward, he grabbed some of the hair that Michael had been holding out of the way, tugging it firmly, as if to remove her mouth from the other man's swollen organ.

Afraid her teeth would injure the delicate flesh, she complied, licking and stroking him instead. She enjoyed the taste of the salty ooze, squeezing him to extract more of the precious liquid for her tongue to swipe at playfully.

Michael pursed his lips, his mind slipping into chaos; the couple before him played havoc with his desire to be gentle with the woman he loved. Reaching up, he grabbed her forearms, freeing himself completely, and roughly dragging her forward, out of the reach of the man who had been punishing her from behind.

A sneer curling his lips, Enrique pushed her, helping to guide her, until she sat on the other man and lay forward, her nipples tickled by the hairs of the heaving chest beneath her. He smiled down at her crinkled orifice, applying another squirt of gel before making his way inside her in one quick thrust.

Tori caught her breath as he slid inside her; inhaling sharply, her lungs clamped down and refused to take in air. Pushing herself up straight, she wedged her body so that neither of them could move for a moment, her fingers grasping her husband's ribs firmly as she gasped, the pain of the sudden stretching causing her to tremble.

Wrapping her from behind, Enrique held still for a moment, moving his hand up and down the length of her torso before palming her pubic bone and applying pressure to the mounds of flesh that covered it. Soothing and comforting her, he whispered into her neck, "Relax, baby girl; you can do this. Just breathe."

Releasing her when he could feel her respirations returning, he eased her back down, pushing her breasts against Michael's broad chest, and adjusting himself more above her so he could take her in deep, hard strokes. Grinning at the man below him, he drove her with an even rhythm, causing her to moan loudly between them.

Kissing Michael lightly, she felt his hands holding her firmly, and she focused on his warm, moist lips. Gripping the pillow on either side of his head, she continued to cry out; struggling to relax, she accepted them both, and could feel them bumping against one another inside her. Feeling her mate beginning to pant beneath her, she queried hoarsely, "Does it excite you, love?"

His reply a loud groan against her face, his grip on her ribs grew firm, almost painful. His hips pushed up against her, struggling to move. His jaw dropped, he huffed, his earthy noises growing louder when his moment of fulfillment drew near.

"My nasty bitch," Enrique called to her from behind, "My filthy fucking whore."

Michael smiled against her cheek, then kissed her harder, grabbing the flesh of her rounded rear end to announce his release. "Oh my GOD, baby girl, you're so nasty," his sweaty forehead pressed against hers, he gripped her, "I love your nasty," he breathed.

She could feel him pulsing inside her, and Enrique pushed himself in and held still, holding off his own fulfillment. She moaned at the pleasure of Michael's juices being added to hers, nuzzling his neck and breathing against his moistness.

When the undulation had faded away, Enrique adjusted his position again, driving her body hard against the man beneath them. The excitement of his presence drove her over the edge, and she began to cry out, the moment of her own crossing growing near. Grabbing her husband's shoulders, then weaving her fingers through locks of hair, she pushed back against the man who slapped in rhythm with her, almost sobbing at the feel of him.

"Don't stop, baby," she begged, "Please dear lord, don't stop."

Michael's hands found their way to her scalp and pulled her head back, her neck taught so he could nuzzle and bit at it. His breath on her windpipe, he licked at the bands within.

Enrique clawed at her hips when he felt the waves overtake her, her calls loud enough, for a moment he thought of the neighbors. His own time came only seconds after, and once over the top, his tingling hands struggled to hold on until the end. Laying over her back, his chest heaved against her, "Jesus Christ," he panted, his sweat dripping onto her.

Tori could see the smile on Michael's face, pleased that everything had in fact, been ok. Lying between them, she exhaled loudly, cleansing her blood from the thrill of their moment. She loved the feel of their hands as they tempted her tingling flesh, dancing across it and causing her breath to come in uneven gasps of joy.

Her mate's breathing slowing, he felt relieved that it had been so easy in the end. He could feel the other man withdraw from her, the satiated grin still on her lips. Stroking a few loose hairs away from her face, he kissed her, the satisfaction welling inside his chest. He knew it had been their first time, but surely not their last.

Who Cares

Tori's boots stomped loudly on the porch, making her way to the door, and she called over her shoulder, "Come on in, Enrique."

The men were coming up the steps as well, everyone tired from their long trek, having pushed the rest of the way without stopping. Flicking on the light, she chased away the darkness, happy to see that things were pretty much the way they had left them. An elated feeling had settled over her when they hit town, and watching him look around her house brought her immense joy.

Throwing her arms around her mate, she breathed in his ear, "Thank you," as if he had brought home a stray dog for them to take in.

Hugging her tightly, he didn't mind. "You're welcome," he replied, then called out more loudly, "We need to get over to the diner and eat before it closes. Drop your stuff and we'll be back in a bit."

Sliding into their regular booth a few minutes later, Enrique fell in next to the girl, then looked around anxiously, "Aren't they gonna finds the three of us being together a little... odd."

"Who cares," Tori sighed, looking at the outline of her shop in the dim glow of the street light. "I love you both, and what are they going to do about it." Her admission tumbled out before she could stop it, followed by a soft flush as she

183

grinned. "You know what I mean," she recovered after a moment.

Trish noticed them a moment later and dashed over to welcome them. Taking the lead, Michael introduced the other man, "Trish this is Enrique. I don't know if you remember the last time he was here," he pointed with an open palm. "He didn't get to stay long then, but I'm pretty sure he's a new resident in town."

If she had any negative thoughts about his arrival, she kept them to herself. Taking their orders, she made for the kitchen to put them in, and busied herself with preparing to close.

"See, that wasn't so hard," Tori joked, smiling at the man next to her.

Back at their dwelling a short time later, their bellies were full and Tori could feel the exhaustion taking its hold on her. Giving the newest member of their family a brief tour, she led him through the large dining area that stood in the center of the first floor, and the kitchen that sat in the back. "We were working on this part when we got the call about the band," she explained the cluttered appearance.

Leading him up the stairs, which faced the front door, she pointed out the bedrooms that sat to the right, "The front is the master, and these other two are nice sized. This one is the nursery," she stepped into the closest one.

"The nursery?" Michael exclaimed, "When did you decide this?"

"When I got my first period," she breathed, looking around at the peeling paint. "I thought I would have plenty of time to fix it up though, before we needed it."

"We have time," Enrique smiled, "I like this place. So's the other bedroom mine?"

"Actually," Michael interceded, "I've been thinking about that. There are two more bedrooms on the third floor.

You and I should each take one, and let her have the master."

"You're gonna make me sleep alone?" Tori gasped, causing her mate to chuckle.

"I doubt you will ever sleep alone, baby girl," he shook his head. "I want us each to have our own space. I know things are all shiny and exciting right now, because it's all new, but trust me... this is going to take some getting used to. And you're right," he tossed his chin at the other man, "There are some people in this town who're going to look down on us."

"Really," Enrique's grin was almost evil, "We could have some fun with that."

"Well, if you guys are taking the bedrooms upstairs, you won't be doing it tonight. The other bedroom, in the back, is made up since we stayed in it while we cared for Marge," she smiled, waving her hair about as she sauntered down the hall. "Or you can sleep in the master with me," she teased. Trailing after her into the larger, front bedroom, Michael's prediction that she wouldn't sleep alone proved to be true, as the three of them shared a bed for the second night in a row.

The following morning, Tori rose early and went for a run, eager to get back into somewhat of a routine. Opening the back door an hour later, she found Enrique preparing breakfast, while her husband made a list of supplies. "Where did you get the food?"

"It was in the cooler," Enrique supplied, "I guess your brother left it here. I gave 'em the float test, and they're still good." Glaring at the eggs fondly, she sufficed herself by making dry toast after checking the loaf for mold, deciding it to be the safer of the two.

"You know it won't last forever," her husband teased.

"What won't," she replied, locating a bottle of water in the fridge.

"The morning sickness. It does go away eventually," he

smiled, trying to encourage her.

"Seems more like all day sickness to me, but that's good to know," she nodded, peering over at his list. "You guys already have plans for the day?"

"Yeah," Enrique placed Michael's plate in front of him. "We're gonna clean out those bedrooms upstairs and gets us situated, then we'll gets started on that room you wanted for the nursery."

"Hey, don't get ahead of yourselves," she tore at her bread. "I don't go to see the doctor for a few days, and I still have a bad feeling about this all working out."

"Oh, you and your bad feelings," Michael chided. "It's fine. I hope it's a boy. I always wanted a son," he tossed at her with a grin.

Tori only shook her dark waves, "You guys can do that then. I'm going down to the shop to have a look around. I'll be back for lunch." Leaving her men to their agenda, she quickly showered and changed, eager to see her tools and put everything back in order.

Going in through the office door in the back, Tori frowned at the layer of dust that covered the interior. *Damn, we left in such a hurry, we didn't cover anything.* Rolling up the front door, she got to work, enjoying the cool morning air, and starting with her tools on the counter in the back.

Hearing a man clear his throat, she turned, expecting to discover Enrique or Michael in the doorway. Instead, she found herself face to face with a short, stubby guy, wearing a long coat. She held her hand up to protect her eyes, struggling to make out his features with the glare of the sun behind him. "Hello?" her voice soft, but warm as she smiled, "What can I do for you?"

Stepping towards him, she lowered her arm slowly, staring at the hand he held extended towards her, and the pistol that was in it. "Who are you?"

"Who I am doesn't matter," he replied. "Your presence has been requested, and that's what does."

Flicking her eyes up to his face, she breathed, "You from The Organization?" She slid her ring calmly off her finger and placed it in her jacket pocket, detecting the gentle tinkle as it dropped against the little silver key.

"I wouldn't ask too many questions," he replied curtly. "I'm to bring you in alive if I can," he chuckled, "Or leave your body here if I can't"

"What about the town?" she shuffled her feet, moving closer to him, laying the two items onto the seat of the bike in front of her nonchalantly. "If I go quietly, you'll leave them alone?"

"Of course," her assailant raised his chin, "Things always go smoother when you cooperate."

Tori swung her gaze around the small space, "Alright. Do I need to bring anything?" she continued to stall.

"No," he informed her flatly. "Walk outside and get in the backseat. Don't touch anything, and don't talk to anyone."

Moving to do as instructed, she strolled out front to find a small, late model sedan parked next the old pump area, another man sitting behind the wheel. Climbing in behind him, the fat man indicated for her to slide across, and he took the seat behind the driver before they drove away.

"Heads up!" Michael called loudly, dropping another armful of debris down the stairs.

"Got it," Enrique replied, kicking it over into their growing pile. "Their family didn't wants none o' this stuff?" he wafted his hand around when he reached the top of the stairs.

"They looked it over after she died," Michael coughed

into his fist. "They took a few things, but the rest is junk. We can toss it."

A few minutes later, Enrique resumed the conversation, "I actually need to talk to you about something, so's I'm glad she's down to the shop. It's kinda for a surprise."

"Ok," Michael glanced over at his new friend, "What's up?"

"I was wondering if you would mind if I gave Tori a ring," the dark-haired man stood still, studying him as he spoke.

"A ring?" he stopped moving, wiping at the sweat on his upper lip, "She already has a ring."

"I know," Enrique shrugged. "The one you gave her, and I'm fine with that. I don't wanna detracts from what it means to you because it means a lot to her too. I wanted to give her one of my own, so that she understands how much she means to *me*."

Michael stared at his counterpart, "I get it. And I really do understand," he began moving again, focusing on the project for a moment. "I don't care if you give her another ring. You could get one that matches ours for yourself, as far as I'm concerned. Whatever you decide, I'll back you."

"You don't thinks that would be weird, us having rings that matched?" Enrique stared at him, his jaw hanging and waiting for the reply.

"Why would it be weird?" Michael countered, keeping his hands busy, "You and I are connected through her. I mean, we can't both be married to her... the law doesn't allow that. But we can both love her, and who says that one of us loves her more? Who says that one of us matters more?"

A long silence followed, Enrique too stunned for words. Eventually, he found his voice, "I really appreciates that, Mike. You have no ideas how much it means to me."

"Actually, I do," he finally made eye contact, his own feelings lurking in his brown orbs. "This situation could so easily be the other way around, Enrique. I would be a fool to not see how it is."

Working side by side, they continued to bag up the loose portions and old clothing, assessing the condition of the furniture when they were done clearing it. "You gettin' hungry yet?" the dark-haired man finally asked. "My eggs are long gone."

"Yeah," Michael brushed at his clothes, "Let's head down to the shop and get her. I'm sure she's not thinking about lunch; forgets everything when she gets into her bikes," he grinned.

Arriving at the garage, the pair parked their rides next to hers, making their way through the wide open door. Placing his shades in his pocket, Michael's gaze swung around slowly, searching the empty space. Making his way through the office, he arrived in the yard and stared at their first home. "Maybe she had to go pee."

"Hey Mike!" Enrique's voice sounded almost shrill.

"What?" Michael replied calmly, moving to rejoin him. Arriving back in the shop, he could see Enrique's palm extended towards him, two shiny silver items resting upon it. "Where'd you get that?!?" his voice also became raised.

"It was sitting heres on the seat," Enrique poked the leather, "Is that the key she told Eli she must have lost; you knows, when they took our stuff?"

Michael lifted the ring to peer inside, and finding the inscription. "Yes, it is. And this is her wedding band. No way this's laying here by accident," his breath grew shallow, the panic beginning to set in.

"You think she took off?"

"Not without help," he reached over, taking the key and holding it up to the light, "Her bike is sitting outside. This is a signal. This key is from The Organization. That's where she is; they have her."

Enrique pursed his lips, not so eager to jump to conclusions, "I'm not so sure that's what it means."

"That's fine," Michael replied, pocketing the items. "Stay here if you want, see if she comes back. Me, I'm going after her."

Looking around in bewilderment, Enrique shrugged to himself, then caught the rope to close the door to the shop. Climbing onto his bike, he kicked it over and headed after the other man, who had gotten a head start. Running up the stairs to their home, he called loudly, "Waits for me. What are we taking?"

Enrique found him standing beside the bed in the master bedroom; Tori's pack lay scattered on top of it. Picking up her pair of knives, Michael turned one in each hand, noticing her name engraved in one of them. "She's defenseless," he breathed. Looking into the eyes of the other man, "We have to help her." Holding out one of the weapons, "You want this?"

"Yeah, I'll take it," Enrique shoved it in his pocket. Picking up her nine, he dropped the clip out to find it full, "I'll take this, too," and shoved it in as well. "We need clothes?"

"Only if they're packed and ready," Michael shook his brown curls, dashing back down the stairs to lock the back door. "The Feds took all our shit. All our intel on them," he lamented when he arrived back at the front door.

"It's ok," Enrique countered, "We know where they's at, more or less. We go to El Paso, then over to Juarez if we have to, and look around. Maybe check out that bar where all those girls was taken from."

"Good plan," Michael agreed. "Let's get out of here," and he locked the front as well. Climbing on their bikes, he zipped over to the diner to inform Trish that they were off again for a few days, knowing she would worry if he didn't.

Riding side by side, it seemed a long journey, making their way north and west until they finally hit Interstate-10. On the major highway, they were able to move faster, arriving in El Paso in time to see the sunset. Stopping for fuel, Enrique inquired as to their next move, suggesting they needed to locate the bar.

"I have the address," Michael reminded him, "I helped Eli plot it on the map, remember?"

"Oh, yeah," his counterpart grinned nervously, "We're gonna get her back. And I think we should call Eli, and let him know what's happened."

"You have his number?" Michael, glanced over, finished filling his tank.

"Yeah," Enrique waved his little phone. Making the call, he hung up a few minutes later to give his partner a rundown, "Basically, he's pretty pissed we didn't calls him sooner. But, he's gonna contact anyone that might be able to help us, and we're supposed to check in if anything changes."

"Good enough," Michael agreed, swinging his leg over his bike, "Let's get to that bar and see what we can find."

Snaking through the streets, they arrived at the club, parking down the block. As they strode to the front, Enrique observed, "Man, this place's huge."

"Yeah," Michael agreed. "Must be how they're able to have their choice of girls here. Let's get inside, get us some seats. We'll order beers and have a look around."

Following the plan, Enrique grabbed a table, and they ordered two bottles from the waitress. Keeping his eyes on the room, he took a long swig, recalling that they never did eat lunch. "You see anything yet?"

Michael shook his head, noticing the door next to them was a bathroom. "On second thought, maybe," and he indicated the portal.

"It's the John," Enrique muttered, "So what?"

"I swear I've seen at least two people who went in, who did not come back out," he looked away, hoisting his beer. "Either it's not really a toilet, or there's another exit from it."

Enrique stared at him, "You're wife's missing, and that's the best you can come up with? The shitter has another way out?"

Michael cut his eyes over at him, "Keep your voice down. This is their turf, remember?"

The other man looked annoyed, impatient as ever, "Wells, I'm gonna take a piss." Standing, he ambled into the men's room, returning a half a minute later.

"Did you even wash your hands?" Michael quipped in disgust.

"No," Enrique shot back, keeping his voice low, "I think I found the exit, and you're not gonna believe it. You still gots that key?"

"The filing cabinet key?"

"Yeah, only that's not what it opens. When you gets inside, there's a grate on the wall, under the sinks. It has a little silver lock on it, and there's cool air coming out of it."

Michael almost spit his beer, "You mean the air conditioner?"

"No, dumbass," he clenched his teeth, straining to keep his voice low, "The opening is about three foot by three foot. It's gotta be a door. Go check it with the key!"

Michael took another slow sip, staring at his friend. Setting his bottle on the table, he called loudly, "My turn," and pushed his way through the entrance. Sure enough, there beneath the sink lay a large cover made of expanded metal. Dropping quickly, he applied the key.

Emitting a small gasp, he pulled the door wide and shoved his head inside, peering into the shaft that dropped almost straight down. Inspecting the miniature door, he discovered a latch to lock it from the other side. Wriggling in, he pulled it closed, sliding his way into the tunnel.

Hidden Paths

Tori sat watching the sunset, sipping from the glass of water that had been placed before her. Casting a glance around her, she could see that she what looked to be Rico's estate, judging from the fine furnishings and the oversized pool. Heaving a deep sigh, she called to the man over her shoulder, who had been watching her, "You got anything to eat around here?"

Her guard only stared at her, not making any effort to reply. Tori leaned back into her chair in disgust, kicking her feet straight out in front of her. *Sorry bastards; I haven't eaten anything but dry toast all fucking day.*

A few minutes later, a tall, slender Hispanic male joined her, wearing a white suit and a straw hat. Tori stared at him as he made his way up to the table, fairly certain that he was the owner of the property. "Hello, Mrs. Anderson," Ruben Ramirez greeted her with a smile that was too large for the occasion.

Raising her chin, the girl didn't bother with pleasantries, "Would you like to explain why I'm here?"

Wafting his hand around his beautiful yard, he laughed, "Isn't this a nice place for a visit?"

"I'm not in the mood for a visit," she replied. "I'm tired and I'm hungry."

The smile disappeared from his lips, and he took a seat at the table next to her. "You should be careful. I only have so much patience."

"Is that a threat?" her voice remained calm.

"I don't make threats," he countered. He pointed a finger at her, crossing his right leg over the left, "Perhaps you need to learn some manners. People who talk to me the way you do don't live very long."

Tori lifted the glass, finishing off the water and chewing the remainder of the ice. "If I wasn't hungry, I might be in a better mood," her stomach lurched and she felt the familiar wave of nausea, followed by dizziness. Placing her elbows on the table, she rested her head in her hands.

"Are you not feeling well?" her captor asked, a faint laugh rolling out.

Tori cut her eyes over at him, then shifted to stare at the glass, *oh my God; he poisoned me.* "What was in it?" she asked calmly.

"Oh, a little something to help you relax," he grinned. "We'll talk about it more when you wake up."

Enrique tapped his empty bottle on the table, debating if he should order another. Continuing to take in his surroundings, he jumped when Michael unexpectedly reappeared beside him. "Get us another round," he commanded, retaking his seat. "And see if they have anything to eat."

Enrique moved to comply, returning a few minutes later with a basket of pretzel and peanut mix, along with two more frosty bottles. "Where does it go?" he ask, placing the items on the table.

Michael lifted his drink, using it to shade his lips, "It's a tunnel. It's lighted and goes far beyond what I could see. And it explains how they are able to take people out of here unnoticed. The question is, do we dare go through it."

"Of course we do!" Enrique countered, his cheeks stuffed with nuts, "How else're we gonna find her?"

"We could try locating their houses," Michael thought aloud, "But I think you're right, the tunnel is probably a direct route. The problem is if we run into anyone who doesn't think we belong there."

"Then eat up, and we'll take our chances," the other man agreed.

"Go call Eli," Michael directed, "Tell him there's a tunnel system under the bar and part of the city, and whoever he is sending should come here first. We'll start exploring when you get back."

Grabbing a hand full of the snack, the dark-haired man moved to comply. Returning a few minutes later, he shook his head, grabbing his bottle with a disgusted frown, "It may be hours before anyone gets here."

"Son of a bitch," Michael shrugged. "We can't wait. Right now, we're going in. When we get inside, go straight down. The door has a latch on it, and I'll be right behind you."

Inside the bathroom, they opened the entrance, and Enrique slid in first, Michael following closely behind. Moving through the narrow space, they had traveled about thirty feet before it opened up into a wider passage. Able to stand upright, he extended his arms, "Hey, Mike; look at this. How long you figure they been diggin' on this?"

"I dunno," he shrugged, tilting his head back to look at the ceiling above them, "About thirty years would be my guess." The tunnel extended in two directions from that point. Using the bar above them to get his bearings, "That way is south, and this way is north," he pointed down the tunnel. "I say we go this way, first. We can always turn around if it meets a dead end."

"Don't say dead," Enrique cautioned.

"Right," Michael grimaced, leading the way.

A few hundred yards down, a smaller tunnel came in from the left. Stretching, Michael couldn't see anything in the pitch black leading up and away from the main shaft. "What do you think? We see what's up there?"

"Might as wells."

There were small steps etched into the dirt floor, making the climb somewhat easier as they felt their way along the walls. A few minutes later, they had reached the top, and a faint light could be seen around the edges of a flat level door above them. "I bet it's in the floor of whatever this is above us."

"Yeah, I think sos too," Enrique reached up to touch it, finding nothing on his side. "It's wide enough to climbs through. Is there a latch on your side?"

Feeling along the rough surface, Michael inhaled several times, trying to calm his nerves, "Found it. Slide back down a bit, and I'll push it open. Nice and slow," he added. Lifting on the door, he discovered that it was spring loaded, and swung wide very easily once he gave it a shove.

Climbing up, he could tell it was a closet, with a barren bedroom through the doorway. "Come on," he called softly behind him, still wanting to be quiet, in case the house wasn't empty.

Once the two of them were topside, they were able to look out of the window, noting that they were in a residential neighborhood. Peeking through the entrance to the room, they made their way quietly through the house, and Enrique drew the nine, in case they needed it. Exploring the structure with the light from outside, they refrained from turning on lights, which would expose their presence.

One of the bedrooms held a sleeping pallet on the floor, which was empty, and there was a small amount of food in the kitchen. Other than that, the house was barren. "What do we do now?" Enrique queried, returning the pistol to his pocket.

"We go back into the tunnel," Michael supplied, "And keep trying doorways until we find the right one."

"Should I check in with Eli again?" Enrique continued to let the other man make the calls.

"And what good is that going to do?" Michael quipped. "They're not here. We're here, and it's taking too long for them to do anything as it is."

Enrique raised his hand, pointing his finger at him and preparing his argument, when the front door to the house swung open, and a young man walked into the deserted living area, carrying a few bags of groceries. Leaping to the side, the two men prepared to confront him, Michael slipped on his shades, anticipating the moment the lights would blaze on.

Startled at the sight of them, the boy gave a yelp, dropping his bags and bolting towards the front door before the men caught him, throwing him to the floor. Straddling him, Michael began to beat him about the face and ears, unleashing his rage.

"That's enough!" Enrique finally called loudly. "Let's see what he knows."

Standing, Michael dragged the man up, into a seated position, "Where does that tunnel go?" he demanded loudly.

Their victim looked back and forth between them, obviously stunned that they knew about the passageway. Punching him in the face, the fairer haired man asked again, this time in Spanish, which earned him a weak response, "It goes everywhere."

"Yeah, no shit. We saw how long it is. We wanna know where it ends." Michael was grasping at straws.

"No," Enrique cut in, "We wanna know which one will take us to Rico."

"Rico?" the boy repeated in bewilderment.

"Yeah, Rico," he twirled his hand in a circular motion, "The head guy. The one who runs the show. Rico Ramirez."

The boy only stared at him. Reaching into his pocket, Michael pulled out Tori's knife, glancing down at her name etched in the metal; *she was much cooler about this shit than I am.* Popping the blade, he laid down his threat, "Talk to me God damn it! Where's my wife!?! Or I'm gonna slit your scrawny throat."

"He can't talk if you slits his throat," Enrique countered, prepared to inflict torture instead.

"Shut up!" Michael bellowed, "Where do they take the girls?"

The young man's eyes glimmered with recognition, "You want the girls?"

"Yes," his voice dropped to a more comfortable level, "Where do they take the girls?"

Standing, the boy scrounged for paper and a writing item, drawing a line, with numerous others coming off of it, like a tree branch. "That's the tunnel," Michael pointed at the map.

"Si, Senor. Is the tunnel." Pointing to the side tunnels, he marked one with a circle, "Girls go here."

Michael lifted the map, his pulse in his throat, "We can't leave this kid here. He'll run off and tell someone that we're down there."

"You gonna kills him?" Enrique suggested in the form of a question.

Michael stared at the brown eyes that were still as wide as saucers. He had been upset with his bride at how easily she had made the call. Now it was his turn. "We take him with us. He gives us any trouble, we slit his throat and leave him." Grabbing the kid's arm, he guided him to the bedroom and the closet that contained the trap door, "Go on, Enrique. We'll put this guy between us."

Instead of following, the boy swung around, taking a swing at the man behind him. In a flash, Enrique had his blade open and took him down. "Next time, don' hesitate," he chided. "It's thems or us, and I prefer thems."

"Yeah," Michael agreed, "Let's go see if he lied on his map." Climbing back into the tunnel, he oriented the sheet of paper, and they retraced their steps, passing the one that led to the bar.

To his surprise, he could hear the sound of the music above them. "Nice. Let's hope he was telling the truth." Counting the side passages as they passed them, they soon arrived at the correct one, guessing they had gone close to a mile from the previous location. Climbing up the miniature staircase, they arrived at another flat surface above them, this time the light around the cracks much brighter.

Pausing, inhaling slowly, Michael could tell the structure above them was occupied, the sound of voices filtering through. Sliding down, he breathed quietly, "We have to go in. I'll open the door to see if I can peek first. Hang back if you want, barge in if you think it will help."

"Sure thing, Mike," Enrique held his position.

Turning the clasp and pushing on the cover, Michael eased his head up, only moving enough to get his eyes above the level of the floor. Seeing only one man, with his back to him, he pushed the door on over, waving to the man behind him and entering the room with a small bound.

Unleashing the knife with a crisp pop, he finished his target with a single motion, Enrique coming in behind him and surveying the space. The voices were coming from down the hall, and the pair moved quickly, spreading through the house and killing every man they found.

Arriving in the last room, they found a girl tied to a bed and gagged. Enrique's heart froze at the sight of the sheets soaked in blood. His hands fumbled, grasping at the dark head of hair and pulling her face around to look into her crystal blue eyes. "It's not her!" he screamed at the man who had begun cutting away her bindings.

"What?" Michael looked over at him with wide eyes.

Enrique ran his thumb under the smooth skin of her left cheek, "It isn't her," he breathed. Turning, he commanded, "Cuts her loose, and we'll lets her go. We still have to find Tori, and this isn't the right house."

Pulling the gag from her mouth, he soothed, "Sshhshsh. It's gonna be ok. We're gonna lets you go." Unleashing his blade, he cut the thin rope that held her hands above her head, becoming aware that she wanted to speak. Leaning closer, he could barely make out her words.

"Hey, Mike," he breathed, "I think she knows where Tori is."

The girl's blue eyes gleamed as she managed to form the words, "New girl."

"New girl," Michael repeated, leaning across the bed from the far side, "Where's the new girl?"

"Raven tunnel," she breathed.

"Raven tunnel," he repeated, hoping she would explain. Her face twisted in frozen agony, she said nothing more.

"She's gone, Mike," Enrique informed him.

"What? What do you mean gone?" Pushing himself up, he stared down at the unmoving features to see that her eyes were fixed and lifeless. "Oh, Jesus," he fumed, "That's all we get? Raven tunnel?!?"

"Come on," Enrique slapped him on the arm, "Let's get back down below. I thinks I knows what it means."

Storming back through the house, Michael paused, staring at a set of oversized cages, *oh my God!* He had presumed they were for keeping animals when they entered, but he had a sinking feeling they were for something else. "Enrique!" he called sharply. Pointing at the prison when he had his attention, "I think they keep the girls in these. Call Eli again, make sure he gets this place on the list."

The other man agreed, making the call and then announcing he was ready to move back below. Reaching the larger passage once again, Enrique pointed out the small drawings he had noticed etched next to the entrance of the smaller tunnel. "See, Fox Tunnel," he indicated the small red creature.

"Holy shit," Michael admitted, "I didn't even see those. Fuck, man! So which way is the Raven Tunnel?!?"

"Calm down," Enrique directed, "I know you're upset, but you gotta focus. Losin' it ain't gonna help her."

Michael breathed in deeply through his nose, "Yeah," he agreed in a quiet voice, clapping his friend on the shoulder. "Ok, have you seen anything that you would call a 'raven'? I mean, what's it supposed to look like?"

"I dunno," his cohort replied, his eyes looking up at the ceiling, "I wished they left us a map… you know… like the ones at the mall. The ones that say *you are here*."

"Yeah," Michael agreed, "That would've been nice."

Poor Man's Justice

Tori lifted her face slowly, searching through the dark strands of hair that hung in front of it. Peering between the waves, she could make out part of the room before her.

"Hello, beautiful," a voice called softly.

Lifting her head completely, the obstruction fell away, and she could see her hands suspended above her. *My God, no wonder my shoulders ache.* Her wrists bound by leather straps, her body hung from the ceiling, and her feet curled on the floor in her unconscious state. Placing them flat, and standing, she relieved the strain on her joints, still unable to lower her arms completely. *Shorter girls would be left hanging from this thing.*

The man laughed, teasing her, "Didn't you think that was funny?"

She looked around, locating the speaker to glare at him. "What's funny?" she growled. Glancing down at herself, she realized that she was naked, briefly wondering what he had done to her while she had been out. Glaring back at him, she waited for him to respond; *so this must be Rico.*

"You," the smile disappeared. "You're not beautiful. You're an ugly piece of shit!" He rose from the stool where he had been perched, reaching her and slapping her across the face. At her failure to react, he lay into her for several follow-up blows.

Tori set her jaw, closing her eyes and breathing deeply.

The pain he inflicted became a part of her, and she did her best not to utter a sound. *Hang on baby girl; you can't give in.*

Stepping back when his arm grew tired, he scowled at her. "You know," he stated bitterly, "Most girls cry when you hit them. Hurt them enough, and they all do. But not you. Why is that?"

"Because I'm an ugly piece of shit," she replied calmly between labored breaths, "And you gotta do better than that limp dick swing if you wanna impress me."

His laughter rolled again, even louder than before. "You have spirit. I like that." He turned his back on her, making his way over to the bar and pouring himself a drink. "I have to admit; I've been looking forward to meeting you for a while, Tori. And you have not disappointed me."

Returning with his glass, he sat back on his stool. "However, it's time for the games to end. I know that you are the one that has put us in such a bind. What I don't know; is why. Where did you come from? Why are you here?"

Tori stared at him, unwilling to allow him to unnerve her. "You tortured Doug. I'm sure you know why I exist."

"Doug? That sniveling little Fed!" he raised his glass and pointed a finger at her, then swirled his drink. "He told me you would get the better of me, but I hardly think you will be of any consequence."

Tori stared, an evil sneer curling her lips, "Is that so." She flexed her fingers, willing the blood to flow. "You obviously don't believe that."

"And what makes you think I don't believe it?" anger crept into his voice.

"You wouldn't have gone to the trouble of retrieving me, if you did," she hissed. Watching with an unwavering stare, she observed while he finished his beverage and stood, placing the container on the bar.

Turning, he strolled casually up to her, grabbing a hand full of her hair. Pulling it, he forced her head back, so that her face pointed at the ceiling, her neck drawn tight.

Panting, she waited, her mind turning how she could escape. Feeling his lips against the taught flesh that covered her windpipe, her eyes slowly closed, and she waited.

His hands roamed over her body, sliding and grasping. She became aware that her flesh burned with fresh cuts and welts, his fingers moving to toy with her breasts.

"You're awfully tall, for a woman," he breathed against her neck, releasing her hair and allowing her to pull her head up and catch her breath. "I'm going to break you, Tori," he whispered.

"Is that what you want? To own me? To possess… me?" she asked in a low tone, her lower lip began to quiver. When he didn't respond, she tried again, "Why is it that you've brought me here? What do you have to gain?"

"There is nothing to gain. There is no purpose. The only reason," he clasped her nipple, twisting it until she could no longer hide the agony, "Is to punish you. To torture you for as long as I can. Either until we are found, which I doubt will ever happen… or until you die. And I assure you," he placed his mouth close to her ear, his fingers flicking her bruised areola, "It is going to be a slow… painful… death."

Tori closed her eyes, his words fading into a distant murkiness. Struggling, she tried to hold on, but she could feel the darkness creeping in around her. She could hear the sound of blows landing, dimly aware of being struck. Her efforts futile, her consciousness slipped further and further away, until it had been lost completely.

Enrique quickened his pace in an effort to keep up, "You think this'll work?"

"I have no idea," Michael replied, "But at this point, it's all we have." Arriving at the club tunnel, they began the ascent. "When we get outside, you make the call, check in one more time and give them our location. But be quick. The bar will be closing soon."

At the top, Michael peered through the grating, seeing a pair of legs moving inside the stall. Waiting until they had exited, he then turned the latch and pushed the door open. Sliding out onto the floor, he stood, allowing his comrade to join him.

Pushing through the thinning crowd, they picked their way outside. Flipping his phone open, Enrique informed the agent they were back at the bar. Listening for a moment, Michael could see him nodding, and then he ended the call. "They'll be here soon, with a whole swarm of agents. They haven't called in the local police, but I think they may do that as well."

"Great," Michael replied. "But I'm not waiting for them. And I don't think the local police will help. Something tells me this place isn't a secret to them."

Enrique nodded, having had the same idea.

Returning to their table, the pair took up their post as the room cleared, and only a few patrons remained. Eventually, the barkeep would turn on the lights, and begin calling out that it was closing time, and everyone would have to leave. Stepping into the bathroom just before he did so, the two men lowered themselves back into the tunnel to wait. A few minutes passed, and the building grew eerily quiet. Able to exit their hiding place, they found an old man sweeping the floors, a younger one placing the chairs up on the tables.

"Excuse me," Enrique called loudly, slowly easing the pistol out of his pocket and pointing it at the younger of the two, "We need to gets a little information from you."

Michael grabbed two of the chairs, placing them next to

one another and indicating for the two men to sit. Instead, a couple more men came tearing in from the offices down the hall, and the partners found themselves in the midst of a genuine brawl.

Using whatever they could get their hands on as weapons, often down to their bare knuckles, they each allowed their rage to consume them. Pulling her knife, Michael cut and slashed wildly, dimly aware that he couldn't kill them all as he would need at least one to show him the way.

A few minutes later, the group of ruffians had been dispensed, and Enrique grabbed at the old man, laying him out and pressing on his gaping gut. "Which way is Raven Tunnel?" he demanded.

The old man's eyes stared blankly, and he made no effort to respond.

Tired of the fight, and over his need to remain civil, Michael slapped their prisoner in the head, "Talk, you old bastard! Which way do we go to get to Rico's house! And don't pretend you don't know… An old geezer like you, I'm sure you know all about The Organization."

The brown orbs didn't falter, "We don't talk about it." His face remained placid, "Talking gets you killed."

"Well, if you tell me, there's a chance you get to live. Otherwise, you're no use to me, and you *will* die." Michael shifted his gaze over at his cohort, giving him a nod.

On command, Enrique shifted his position, adding pressure to the wound, causing the old man to groan loudly.

The old bastard is tough; he eventually had to admit, when they weren't getting anywhere. "Get off him," he tossed his chin into the air.

The man doubled over in agony but wasn't ready to give up.

Reaching into his pocket, Michael pulled out the wedding

band, shoving it under his victim's nose, "You see this? It belongs to my wife. They took her, and I'm here to get her back."

Holding his gut, the blood oozed across his fingers. Pulling himself up, he snorted, "You'll never get her back. No girls never come out of the tunnel once they go in."

"Just point us which way and we'll sees about that," Enrique challenged.

Staring up at him, "What the hell..." he panted; "It's your funeral. Take the turn to the left. It's a long way down, couple o' miles. Look for the raven, on the left."

As soon as he finished speaking, Enrique finished him off with a final swipe of his blade, muttering, "No loose ends."

Leaving the old man's body where it lay, the pair bolted for the bathroom, sliding into the tunnel once more. They moved quickly, climbing down the narrower portion, and leaping out into the main shaft. Michael in the lead, Enrique followed, calling, "I hope we're not too late."

"We're not too late," the other man replied, "We're going to make it. Have to make it. And you can get your ring, and we can have our baby, and we get to have our lives; whatever we want them to be." He focused on the path ahead of them, rocking his jaw side to side as he thought about all the things that were at stake, and how badly he wanted those things.

Arriving at the designated tunnel, Michael stopped to stare briefly at the small black bird carved into the rock, its wings spread in flight. They climbed quickly, arriving at a normal sized door at the top. Grasping the handle and giving it a turn, Michael cracked it a small amount, peeking out to discover an expanse of grass before him. Pushing it open wider, he stepped out into a garden area.

Turning to gaze around, he noticed that the box that housed the entrance was covered in vines, well hidden once the door had been closed behind them. Moving over, next to the wall of the estate, they remained in the shadows as they continued to peer around and formulate their plan.

"We gets into the house over there," Enrique pointed out the entrance eagerly.

"Yeah," Michael nodded. "You have any rounds left?" he inquired, recalling having heard shots back at the bar.

"Sure, a few," his partner agreed.

"Alright, let's make our way across and get inside. We kill everyone we run into, knives if we can; bullets if we must." He held up his hand, another thought occurring to him, "Send Eli a text; tell him how to locate the right tunnel."

"Ok," Enrique pulled out the phone and typed in the message, then fell in behind him as they moved, keeping to the dark areas as much as possible.

Arriving at the sliding glass door, Michael moved the large pane inside the frame slowly, causing almost no sound. When it had opened about twelve inches, he turned to his side, and they crept in, moving across the tile floor. Looking around, he hoped to locate the security cameras if there were any, but didn't have any luck.

Turning down a hallway on the far side of the room, they wormed their way through the house, pausing periodically to listen to the silence of the massive structure. Finding an indoor pool, they worked their way around it, and were met by a surprised guard, who immediately attacked them.

The pair killed the man with ease, relieving him of his pistol. Holding the weapon in front of him, Michael continued through the corridors, leading the way. Hearing the faintest of cries, he stopped in his tracks, "You hear that?"

"I hears it," the other man replied. "Keep going."

A moment later, they turned a corner, and the scream became a high pitched wail, then cut off abruptly, falling into silence. Panic gripped the two men, and they raced forward, bursting into the room.

Tori hung from metal supports in the ceiling, her arms extended above her. The Ramirez brothers were enjoying their time with her, the sight sending her rescuers into a wild fury.

Taking the two men by surprise, the pair unleashed their fury and flung themselves upon them. Beating them until they could no longer resist, the younger men left them laying on the floor, unconscious and bleeding out rapidly from the holes they had been given.

"We should torture them," Enrique panted when they were broken.

"No, let them die," Michael countered, standing and turning to the girl. Reaching her, he lifted her limp frame, calling loudly, "Get her down. Cut the straps or something."

Enrique used his blade, fighting to push it through the thick leather. When she was finally free, Michael laid her lifeless body on the floor, pushing her hair back away from her face and tracing the line of her scar.

"She's breathing," he whispered, "Call and get us an ambulance. Call Eli, too, and tell him we found her."

Dashing away to locate a land line, Enrique placed both calls simultaneously, straining to maintain his sight on the couple. When he had finished, he grabbed a white linen table cloth and carried it over to wrap her in. "How is she?"

"Bad," came the reply, "She's still unconscious. They hurt her…"

"She's gonna be ok, Mike. We made it. We got our justice. She's been avenged."

"No, this isn't really; poor man's justice maybe. It cost us too much," he adjusted the cloth around her body, noting the dried streaks of blood on her legs. "Please God, let us keep *her*," he begged. *Please, don't take them both.*

Life of Choice

Tori lay still, slowly becoming aware of the ache that seemed to reach every part of her being. *Breathe, baby girl.* She could hear the beeps... distant, but growing nearer. *Oh dear lord, where am I?* Lying still, she continued to force her chest to rise and fall, focused on surviving.

Uncontrollably, her eyes fluttered, and she could hear the voices breaking through the darkness. The sounds of men were coming closer, her flesh burning. Allowing her eyes to open slowly, she stared at the white square tiles above her, *oh my God! I'm in the hospital.* She gasped loudly for air, hot tears burning her eyes and running down her temples.

"Tori?" a male voice spoke, so close and yet so far. "Tori, can you hear me?"

She felt his hand on her arm. Shifting her gaze, she found him. "Eli," she breathed more than she spoke, a small amount of drool oozing from her mouth. Reaching, he brushed her cheek, wiping it away.

"Welcome back!" he called softly, turning to speak to the other man in the room.

Special Agent James Godfry ambled forward, taking his place on the opposite side of the bed. "Hello," the round man said in a hushed voice, "Good to see you alive."

"Am I?" the girl managed, her brain continuing to pick up on more sensations, becoming aware of the hiss of the hose that ran to her nose. Lifting her arm ever so slightly, she

211

detected the tubes, *yup; I'm a mess.* "How did I get here?"

"Michael," Eli supplied, "And I guess Enrique gets some of the credit. They hunted you down. Found where they had taken you, and busted the place up. Literally."

Tori grimaced, unable to produce a real smile. "Are they ok?"

"They're fine," Godfry spoke crisply. "They're outside, along with your band, manager, and God knows who else. You really know how to draw a crowd."

Tori's mouth twitched, not sure how she felt about that. Lying still, she breathed deeply for a few minutes, the two men watching her while she gathered her strength. Eventually, she tried unsuccessfully to sit up.

"Just rest, baby girl," Eli called softly. Leaning forward, he held his face above hers, and she caught a whiff of the gel in his hair. "All you have to do now is heal. There's no more bad guys to tear it all apart," he consoled her.

"Are they really gone?" her words were ragged, her chest heaving.

"Yes, they're really gone," his hand reached to smooth her hair. "You're free, baby girl." He paused, not sure if he could bring himself to push on, not ready to leave her either.

"Am I still pregnant?" her voice remained low, her bottom lip picking up a tremor.

Eli continued to stroke her, "I'm going to let the doctor talk to you about that." He drew in air loudly through his nostrils, "I hear that Enrique has moved in with you and Michael, in that humongous house of yours in Texas." He glanced over at his superior, recalling what he had said about the girl, and her need to be surrounded by men. "I'm sure the rest of the town will be real receptive to that."

"I don't care what they think," she countered, her voice growing stronger. "I'm so lucky, Eli. Some people spend their whole lives, searching for just one person who thinks the world of them, and I found two."

"You found more than that," a tear spilled over before he could catch it. "But we can't all live in that house, hiding from the world."

"There's plenty of room," she beamed for an instant, "If you ever change your mind."

"You know I can't do that," he shook his head slightly, "Your time is over, and you get to rest." He forced himself to smile, "I still have a job to do."

"I know," she blinked up at him, aware that his hand held hers, she gave it a small squeeze.

Standing up straight, he exhaled a large, cleansing breath, wiping at his face. "It's time for us to go, so the others can come in and visit you. They've been on pins and needles since you were brought in, and we shouldn't keep them waiting any longer."

"I need to speak to Danny first, please," she called softly. Looking over at Godfry, she could see him hesitate. "You have something to add, sir?"

"Yes," he placed his hand on the rail, "I wanted to thank you, for what you've done."

"For what I've done?" she stared at him, her eyes growing dark. "It would appear I haven't done anything... except get the shit kicked out of me."

"You've done far more than that, lady. We owe you a debt we can never repay." He smiled, "And we are truly grateful. Your story is still classified... but certain parts have already been leaked, especially what happened with the group, and how you saved everyone during the attack by the Spiders. You are... heroes," he laughed. "Don't be afraid. Tell whatever you are comfortable with, and be proud." Looking over at the man across the bed, he nodded, and the pair made their way to the door.

Closing her eyes, Tori lay quietly, listening to the hiss of her hose and beep of the machines. Focused on breathing, she waited calmly for her brother to join her.

The two federal agents exited the large double doors of the ward, making their way over to the crowd of people gathered around, sitting, standing and worrying. "She's awake," Eli announced. "She wants to see you," he indicated her brother with a nod.

Michael shifted his stance, unsure if he should be upset that she chose her brother first; *he is after all, her family.* Looking over at Enrique, their eyes met, and he could tell he had been thinking the same thing. "Relax," he spoke softly to the other man in their mutual tongue, "We'll get our turn."

"Yeah, we will," his friend agreed, "And I'll take whatever I can get."

Michael grinned broadly, "I know that's right. We both will."

A man in a blue lab coat joined them, holding out his hand, "Mr. Anderson? I'm Dr. Hubbard, Tori's attending physician. If you would like to step over this way, we have much to discuss."

"Oh, no," he shook his sandy curls, flicking his brown orbs at the other man, "Whatever it is, please share. I don't think I love her any more than everyone else here does. She's pretty special."

The doctor cast his eyes around the group, mouth open slightly, "Well, alright." He nodded faintly, still addressing the man he had intended to confer with, "Your wife is in pretty rough shape. She has a few fractures and has sustained numerous internal injuries."

Michael nodded uncontrollably, "Yeah, she was pregnant, too."

The doctor inhaled through his wide nostrils, "Well, she still is pregnant."

The group gasped in unison, their mumblings of joy and

relief overlapping into a wave, rising to a small peak, and then falling away. "That's not all," Michael supplied. "She has some complications and will have to see her regular doctor when we get her home."

"You mean Dr. Lazenby," Dr. Hubbard supplied. "Yes, I've already conferred with him, and we did a few tests while she was unconscious. She does not have Asherman's Syndrome that we could detect. Her pregnancy risk is somewhat elevated due to her recent encounter, but no more than any other woman's would be."

"You means she's gonna have the baby?" Enrique moved forward, standing closer to Michael.

"Yes," he nodded confirmation. "I mean, with every pregnancy, there is always risk, but she has the same chance as anyone else. If she takes care of herself, there isn't any reason why she can't carry the child to term."

The two men flung their arms around one another, smacking each other on the back. "You hear that?" Michael beamed, "We get to finish that nursery after all."

"Yeah we do," his counterpart agreed, slapping his friend's shoulders before dropping his hands back to his sides. "Anything else we needs to know?"

"Only that she should remain here for a few days. And after that, she's going to need some time to heal, but she will probably make a full recovery."

"So, she could rejoin the band, if she wanted," Cody interceded.

"Theoretically, she can do whatever she wants to do; all she has to do is choose," the physician supplied. "Now, I do have other rounds to make, if you will excuse me," he nodded at the group and took his leave.

As soon as he was gone, Enrique pushed on his friend's arm and they moved away to put their heads together, "Listens, uh; Are you guys sures about me... and you... an' her?"

Michael laughed, "Ricky, don't make me whoop your ass." Cutting his eyes over at him, he continued to grin, "You're free to go, but you and I both know she wants you here," he nodded. "And I want you here. There isn't any reason any of us has to suffer, anymore."

"Ricky?" his dark brown eyes shone brightly.

"Yeah," Michael pursed his lips, suppressing his grin for a moment, "That's your new nick name."

"I has a nick name; Tori calls me *baby*," he grinned.

"Yeah, well, I'm not calling you *baby*," he reached over to give his counterpart a friendly punch in the bicep.

Taking a moment to think, Enrique toyed with his lips then professed, "I guess we're set."

"We're set; she needs us both, brother," Michael offered him his hand again, ending with a half hug and heartfelt slap on the back.

Watching the door to the hallway that led to her room, the pair waited eagerly until Brian exited the wide portal, making his way across to the group. "She wants to see you," he pointed at his brother-in-law, holding a straight face and not giving anything away.

Looking over at his roommate, Michael grinned, "You ready?"

"I don't think she meant both of you," Brian's voice held an edge.

Enrique nodded, ignoring the jab, "Yeah, I'm ready," following his friend.

Michael entered the tiny room, his breath hanging in his chest, "Hi." He hung back, taking in the sight of her half reclined position, and the myriad of wires and machines, while Enrique stepped in beside him.

"Hi," she breathed back at him, scratching at the tube in her nose, the bruises on her face hiding her features in the dim light. Noticing the second man, a slow smile curled her lips, "I hear the pair of you worked together… to save me."

Michael crept forward, taking the near side of the bed while Enrique took the far, placing her between them.

"Yeah, we were quite a team," her husband beamed across her body. Reaching down, he used gentle fingers to situate her connections and locate her hand. Dropping to his knees next to her, his head lay over onto the metal, and he pressed his free thumb into his eye.

"Are you crying?" she stared at his sandy curls.

"Yeah, well, you know, men have tears, too," he sighed loudly, wrapping her digits between his two palms.

"Are you going to cry?" she whispered, reaching for the dark haired man to her right.

"Naw," he gave her a slight shrug, entwining his fingers with hers, "I'm good," followed by a slight grin. "Not gonna asks how you feels, though."

"Thanks," she managed a weak grimace, "I must look pretty awful."

"No, love," Michael smiled as well, "You look pretty good, considering you've just cheated death for the second time."

The three grew quiet for a moment, listening to the sounds of the machines, an inner warmth encircling the trio in the cool air of the room.

"So, what's the plan, baby girl?" Enrique reached to smooth her hair, leaning over her to get closer.

"There is no plan, baby." Her movements were small, obviously in pain, "And I'm not in charge. This isn't a crew. This is a family, and we decide things together."

Instantly, he could feel the burn in the back of his throat, and the tickle in his own eyes and nose. "Shit," he caught the droplet as it reached his stubble, and she giggled slightly before she winced in pain.

"I win," she professed.

"Oh, is this a game?" Michael lifted his hand, sliding it over onto her belly. "Momma don't play fair," he said in a soft voice.

"Momma?" her blue eyes grew misty, "You mean…?"

Enrique beamed, "Yeah, everything's fine. The Doctor said you should haves the baby without any problems."

"Oh my God!" she pulled both her hands free to cover her face, her own droplets stinging her cheeks. The two men shared a knowing glance as she inhaled deeply, "Does Danny know?"

"Your brother? No," Enrique looked confused, "Well, he might knows now, he was in here when they told us."

The girl pulled her hands down slowly, "He's pretty upset with me at the moment, I think."

"And why's that?" Michael continued to run his hand over the blankets.

"Because I'm going back to Texas," she replied in a low tone, "Forever."

"You quits the band?" Enrique held a dazed expression.

"Yeah, I did," she tried to sit up a little more, then sank back into the mattress, "I don't like being famous. I love to play my guitar, don't get me wrong, and I may write songs for them, or who knows… But like I told him… I miss our quiet lives in that little town." Her smile grew wide again as she reached towards the dark haired man, "I really hope you're going home with us, too."

"Of course I am," he swallowed noticeably. "What else am I gonna dos, go hang out with Brett?"

"No, baby," she giggled, lifting her other hand to brush Michael's curls. "Wow. All in all, I guess this is the perfect ending then, isn't it." She heaved a loud sigh, "We all get to be happy."

"Oh, no, baby girl," Michael shook his sandy hair, "This

isn't the end." He laughed aloud, looking boldly over at the man across from him, recalling how much his world had changed in the year that he had really known her. "Whatever life lies beyond these walls, is ours for the taking, because this," he paused, shifting his gaze to her, "This has only been… the beginning."

About the Author

Anyone who knows me could tell you, I am a friendly kind of person, never met a stranger and take up conversations anywhere at any time. I work hard, and my mind never seems to shut down, as I wake up often in the middle of the night with ideas pouring out and demanding to be dealt with. Of course that means much of my books were written in the middle of the night.

I grew up and still live in the great state of Texas where everything is bigger, where we have warm weather and a central location. I love my state, my town, and my family, which includes my four sons, my significant other, and many friends as well.

I have thoroughly enjoyed writing this story and hope that you will love reading it just as much. And of course, there will be many more adventures to come.

You can follow Samantha Jacobey at:
Website: www.SamJacobey.com
Facebook: https://www.facebook.com/SamJacobey
Twitter: https://twitter.com/SamJacobey
Pinterest: http://www.pinterest.com/samanthajacobey/

Acknowledgements

Well, you have reached the end of my story, such as it is, and I hope that you have enjoyed reading it as much as I have loved sharing it. I would like to take a moment to thank a few people. These are my dearest friends and greatest supporters, and they have helped me more than words can express as I have traveled along my fantastic journey; but I would like to try.

Don – the significant other who has never read a single page of my work, but has supported me in a magnitude beyond expression. Thank you for listening, sharing, and providing for me so that I am free to follow this dream. You truly are the love of my life.

Derek – thank you for being the first to read and give feedback on my books. Your insight was helpful, but I was encouraged more by the fact you wanted to read about my characters than anything else. You will always be my chief editor and dearest friend across the pond.

Lori – the PA I could never afford if I paid you what you are worth. You truly are the glue that binds my team, and keeps me on track with all the deadlines, dates, and engagements. I have come a long way since we met, and I know that I owe a great deal of that success… to you.

Kim – I could not have chosen a better assistant and no day goes by I don't thank God for you. Always willing and able, your creativity and devotion have moved me deeply. Your visuals draw people in, and we are growing because of your efforts; thank you for your support.

Jamie and *Brenda* – you are fantastic pimpers, and I appreciate you taking over the street team and helping to make it so successful. Your creativity takes my breath away, and I thank each of you for all the time you put in, supporting my work and getting my name in front of readers.

Melissa and *Alice* (and the rest of my power pimpers) – your dedication is phenomenal! You put me out there every day, and you make such a difference. Thank you for your time and energy.

Nicolene, Heather, Michelle and *Joely* (and any others who have chipped in along the way) – you are very talented ladies, and I thank you from the bottom of my heart for all the wonderful visuals you have so graciously created for me.

The Crazy Lady Authors (Stalkers) – you are the best friends a girl could have. Thank you for your love and support, and some day we are going to hold a signing that is for all of us - together, strong, and proud. To my sisters, I wish you all the very best.

Sam's Sassy Bitches – you guys are the best street team and fan club I could ever hope to have. Your love and support mean worlds to me, and if I could call you out individually by name, I would. You do a fantastic job of sharing and supporting. I appreciate each and every one of you very much.

And finally, to the rest of my *followers, fans* and *reviewers* – thank you so much for your time, love, and response. Your words are greatly appreciated, your opinions always noted, and your time never wasted. I hope you have genuinely enjoyed my work, and I look forward to sharing more stories and adventures with you in the days and years to come.

Other works by Samantha Jacobey

http://www.amazon.com/-/e/B00GEB5LX0

Summer Spirit Novella Series - no one EVER had a summer romance like this… Charlie visits another plane, parallel to our own, where Summer Angels and Dark Angels battle over the fate of man. A unique twist on an old idea that will keep you guessing; will Charlie and Clarisse ever find their HEA? (New adult)

Irrevocable Series – from affluent beginnings, BAILEY DEWITT's life has become a broken mess... after her parents died unexpectedly, she didn't think it could get any worse. But when the arrogance of man catches up and puts the entire world into a dooms-day spiral, there will be only ONE PLACE she can run to... the ONE PLACE she wanted desperately to escape.... (New Adult)

Teach Me to Prey – in this standalone thriller, JASON TRUITT and his friends have gotten their way for years. Deceit, sex, and foul play aren't normally covered in the curriculum, but they're doing whatever it takes to get under BECKY STEWART's skin. When one of the boys turns up dead, it's a race against time to save the others; a STUNNING STORY that will get your heart racing and leave you breathless by the end… (New Adult)

The Wicked Awakened – a Halloween novel, a five hundred year old witch wants to turn SARAH MATTHEWS' body into her new home… A twisted tale involving a coven hell bent on seeing that she succeeds. Who will come out on top in this epic battle of wills? (Mature read, 18+ for sexual content and violence)

www.ingramcontent.com/pod-product-compliance
Lightning Source LLC
Chambersburg PA
CBHW030303180626
46810CB00003B/906